Elizabeth Gail and the Mystery at the Johnson Farm

Hilda Stahl

Tyndale House Publishers, Inc., Wheaton, Illinois

Dedicated with love to
Vera and Ed Stahl, Sr.

The Elizabeth Gail Series

Cover and interior illustrations by Kathy Kulin

Juvenile trade paper edition
Library of Congress Catalog Card Number 78-66373
ISBN 0-8423-0739-7
Copyright 1978 by Word Spinners, Inc.
Printed in the United States of America

96   95
13   12

Contents

ONE
A new family

To annoy Miss Miller, Libby snapped her gum louder as she huddled in the corner of the car next to the door. She wouldn't look at Miss Miller. Instead, she watched the telephone poles whiz past.

"I'm sure you'll like it at the Johnsons' farm," said Miss Miller.

Libby was sure she wouldn't. A lump tightened her throat.

Miss Miller sighed. She'd been trying to convince Libby she'd like living in the country. "If you try hard, you'll learn to love the Johnsons. They are good people."

Libby chewed her gum harder, trying to irritate Miss Miller. Libby counted the mailboxes along the long stretch of flat countryside. Five mailboxes, then a turn. Her hands were icy. The muscles tightened in her back and neck, giving her a headache. She wasn't going to love anybody. Not ever again! Especially not foster parents.

"It's only another mile," said Miss Miller, turning

the car heater down to medium. Her fragrant perfume drifted through the car. "I'll be out to see you in two weeks."

"Check up on me, you mean," mumbled Libby, crossing her thin arms and sticking out her pointed chin.

"I didn't mean that at all, Libby, and you know it." Miss Miller slowed the car down and looked hard at Libby. "I do like you, Libby; I want you to be happy."

Libby sat up and looked straight ahead. "I am happy." She chewed her gum even harder and wished she were a million miles away.

"There's the house," said Miss Miller, turning into a long driveway.

Libby's eyes opened wide. What a house! She had never seen such a big, beautiful house in all her life. The lawn stretched from the road to the house and far behind it. Several giant trees, already naked for winter, stood in the yard. Libby felt a tingle of delight as she saw on one of the trees a large swing hooked to a fat branch, the grass worn away from under it. Then the tiny happy feeling vanished and a hard knot settled in her stomach. This was just another foster home filled with strangers.

Miss Miller let in a gust of cold wind as she slid out of the car.

Libby clutched the door handle, looking with embarrassment down at her shabby clothes. She chomped down hard on her gum as she climbed out of the warm car into the cold.

Miss Miller opened the trunk and motioned for Libby to take out her suitcase.

Reluctantly Libby reached for the lone, shabby suitcase, wishing she could sink through the ground.

"So, this is our new girl," cried a tall, good-looking blonde woman, hurrying from the front door of the house.

"Hello, Mrs. Johnson," said Miss Miller, smiling. "Mrs. Johnson, this is Elizabeth Gail Dobbs. We call her Libby."

Libby snapped her gum extra hard. Her heart raced as the blonde woman smiled at her.

"We're glad you're here, Libby."

Suddenly a terrible sound, coming from just behind her, startled Libby. She turned in panic. A large white goose, long neck out, ran honking right at Libby. She screamed. The goose flapped his wings wildly, honking again. Libby screamed again, kicking frantically at the goose. He flew against her, knocking her to the ground.

"Goosy Poosy, you stop it this minute," cried Mrs. Johnson, shooing the goose away and reaching for Libby. "Are you hurt? Goosy Poosy is our pet. He didn't mean to scare you."

Libby's heart beat so fast she couldn't answer back with the angry retort that stuck at the tip of her tongue. She leaped up, out of Mrs. Johnson's reach. Wildly she looked around for the goose. It was standing by the side of the house, eyeing her. Libby swallowed hard, backing against the car.

"He won't hurt you," said Miss Miller, patting Libby reassuringly on the arm.

"Miss Miller, would you like a cup of tea or coffee?" asked Mrs. Johnson, pulling her coat closer around her to shut out the chilly wind.

"No, thanks," she answered. "I must get right back to town. See you in two weeks, Libby."

Libby just looked at her, hoping Miss Miller was feeling really bad for just deserting her on the front yard with a strange woman and a wild goose.

"Good-bye, Miss Miller," said Mrs. Johnson. "Thank you for bringing us Libby." Mrs. Johnson stood quietly until Miss Miller was almost out of the driveway, then she turned to Libby. "Let's hurry in. It's cold out here."

Libby didn't want to walk into the beautiful house. She felt so ragged and dirty. Mrs. Johnson was well dressed and pretty. The wind whipped her blonde hair into a mess, but she didn't seem to mind.

Libby flipped a braid over her skinny shoulder, hating her braids and her ugly clothes and her shabby suitcase. "I didn't want to come live here," said Libby defiantly.

"I can understand that, Libby." Mrs. Johnson stopped outside the door, her slender hand on the knob. "A girl likes to live with her own family. Since you can't we're very glad you can live with us. Ben, Susan, and Kevin are waiting inside to meet you. Susan is excited about having a new sister." Mrs. Johnson turned the doorknob and pushed open the heavy front door.

Libby swallowed her gum as she stepped into the hallway. A grandfather clock bonged four bongs. Libby jumped. She stared around her in fascination. Never, never in her eleven, almost twelve years had she seen such a house. This was a house with a capital H. Libby always put a capital letter on anything that really impressed her. She turned in surprise as Mrs. Johnson introduced her to the three smiling kids.

"This is Susan," said Mrs. Johnson, her hand on the girl's arm.

She said it as if she had something to be proud about, thought Libby as she looked the other girl up and down. They were the same age, but Libby felt like an awkward giant next to the short, fine-boned girl dressed in blue jeans and a faded blue sweatshirt.

"We'll have fun together," said Susan, smiling with pleasure.

"Oh, sure," said Libby with a shrug and a sour look on her thin face. She really wanted to smile and be nice, but she couldn't. She didn't know how. She scuffed her worn sneaker on the plush carpet.

"This is Ben," said Mrs. Johnson, resting her arm on the tall, thin boy beside her. "And this is Kevin." Kevin was short, a little chubby, and wore glasses.

He pushed his glasses hard against his face. "Want to see my pony, Libby?"

Libby almost smiled. A pony! She hadn't expected that. She only shrugged as if it didn't matter if she saw the pony or not.

"I'll take your suitcase to your room and you can go with Kevin and Susan to the barn," said Ben, taking the shabby suitcase from Libby.

Libby looked at him a long time. He was good to look at. She watched until he disappeared up the wide stairs. His hair was red with a capital R. Miss Miller had told Libby that the Johnsons owned the general store in town, but she hadn't told her they had a farm with real animals, especially horses.

"Let's go to the horse barn," said Susan.

"OK," said Libby indifferently. Her heart raced. Finally she'd be close enough to touch a pony. She took a deep breath to push back her excitement. It wasn't safe to get excited over or start liking anything at a foster home. During the past, she'd learned how to behave at foster homes.

TWO
The bedroom

Kevin's pony Sleepy was a nice enough pony, but
Susan's horse was too fabulous for words. Libby leaned
against the stall and looked at the spotted horse.
Susan called it a mare and said her name was Apache
Girl. Libby barely concealed her excitement.

Reluctantly Libby moved away from Apache Girl to
follow Susan and Kevin through the barn. Ben's horse
was all black with a white mark on its face. Ben called
him Star, Kevin told Libby proudly.

Side by side in two stalls were two of the biggest
horses Libby had ever seen.

"They're draft horses. Jack and Dan," explained
Susan, leaning against the stall door. "Dad uses them
to pull the wagon and the sleigh in the winter. He
drives them for parades in town."

Kevin strained to reach one of the draft horses and
patted it. "Ben uses them for his Christmas tree
business."

Libby couldn't hold the question back. "What's a
Christmas tree business?" Then she pretended to lose
interest. She looked at the bales of hay stacked in an

empty stall. A big black cat lay curled on one of the bales.

Kevin answered Libby anyway. "Ben planted Christmas trees all around the back fifty acres of our farm. Each year he takes families in the sleigh or the wagon back to find their own Christmas tree. The family pays for the ride and the tree. Sometimes Mom gives them hot cocoa when they come back."

The thought of riding in a sleigh or wagon behind the beautiful gray horses to get a Christmas tree made Libby shiver with excitement. "I'm cold," she complained to hide her excitement as she pushed her hands into her jacket pockets. "Are we going to stay out here all day?"

Susan looked at her questioningly. "Libby, let's be friends."

"Gonna make me?" snapped Libby.

"No," said Susan, frowning. "Come look at one more mare and then we'll go in."

Libby felt like crying. She wanted to like Susan and have Susan like her in return. Libby knotted her fists tight in her pockets. She absolutely couldn't allow herself to like Susan. It would only make it worse when Libby had to leave.

They stopped beside the last stall. "That's Dad's mare Tessy and her filly Snowball," said Kevin proudly. "Snowball's only a month old."

Libby stared at the adorable white baby, wishing she could put her arms around Snowball and hug her and pet her. Libby had never seen a baby horse before. She closed her eyes tightly and pushed away from the stall. "I don't want to hang around here all day," she said sharply.

14

Susan started to say something, then closed her mouth tight as they left the barn.

Kevin clicked off the lights and closed the door.

The big white goose that had knocked Libby down earler honked and ran toward her. Libby screamed and jumped behind Kevin, hanging onto his shoulders and pushing him between herself and the goose.

Kevin laughed. "Goosy Poosy won't hurt you. He's our pet."

"Meet Libby, Goosy Poosy," said Susan, holding her hands out to the goose. The goose raced awkwardly to Susan and laid its head in her hand. Susan rubbed his long neck. "Libby's part of our family now."

"Rub his neck," said Kevin, squirming away from Libby.

Libby's heart raced. "I won't touch that thing. He might bite." She glared at Susan and Kevin as she hid her hands behind her back. How could they even suggest she touch that terrible creature?

"Just pet him. He's so soft," said Susan, rubbing her hands down the goose's neck.

"You can't make me do anything I don't want to do!" exclaimed Libby belligerently.

"Don't be stupid," said Susan impatiently, her blue eyes meeting Libby's hazel ones. "We thought you'd like Goosy Poosy. We weren't forcing you to do anything."

"I hate living here and I hate you," said Libby, lifting her pointed chin high in the air.

"If you keep on acting like this, we'll hate having you," said Susan angrily.

"Let's go in," said Kevin, shoving his glasses hard against his round face. "Libby, you'll get used to the animals after you've been around them a while. Doing chores every day will help you be friends with them and maybe you'll like it better here."

"Chores!" gasped Libby, her eyes round. "Will I be forced to work outside?" It scared her to think of it. She'd done a lot of hard work in the years she'd lived in foster homes, but it had always been indoor work. How could she possibly do outside chores?

"Are you afraid to work?" snapped Susan, her hands on her hips. "Why, out of all the girls we could have chosen, did we choose you?" Susan raced into the house, slamming the door.

A hard lump filled Libby's throat. Ice settled around her heart. Why did she have to make Susan angry? Susan had been willing to be friends. Now she wouldn't want to talk to Libby again.

"You really made her mad," said Kevin with a sigh as he walked slowly beside Libby toward the back door.

"Good!" snapped Libby. But she didn't feel good about it.

"Susan forgets to watch her temper," explained Kevin, stepping around a small evergreen tree. "Dad told her since she has his red hair, she'd have to fight the temper that goes with it." Kevin laughed. "I get mad too, and look: I don't have red hair. I have blond hair like Mom."

Libby touched her ugly brown braids. She had hair like her mother. Libby's stomach knotted. It had been five years since Libby had seen her mother. She had promised Libby that she could stay with her forever. She'd stayed one month and Mother had run away with that weird man she'd met in a bar, leaving Libby

16

alone until the caseworker had found her. Libby didn't know where her dad was. He'd left Mother and Libby when she was two years old. Libby stifled a moan. It hurt too much to think about her parents.

Libby tugged on a rope handing from a bell near the back door. The bell clanged loudly.

"Don't do that," said Kevin, stopping the bell. "That's used only to call us to the house when we're too far away to hear Mom."

Libby shrugged, flipping the rope high. She opened the back door and stepped into the closed-in porch. The warmth of the house wrapped around her pleasantly.

"Hang your jacket here," said Kevin as he pulled off his jacket and hung it on a hook by the back door.

Libby reluctantly hung up her shabby jacket beside a large red plaid coat. Her mouth drooped. Tears stung her eyes. She wanted to get away from everyone and everything. She tugged impatiently at her baggy cotton dress, wishing she had something to wear that fit her right. Her sneakers were dirty and her socks droopy.

Mrs. Johnson greeted them cheerfully as they stepped into the family room. "Come with me, Libby. I'll show you your room."

Libby kept her eyes on the thick carpet as she followed Mrs. Johnson to the stairs and up.

"I think you'll like this room," said Mrs. Johnson, pushing open the door and letting Libby walk in first.

Libby gasped. Medium pink, dark pink, and red ran riot throughout the room. An entire matched unit of chests, shelves, bookcases, and desk stood against one wall, ending at a corner beside a large window with a window seat. The carpet was dark pink, the walls medium. Libby gingerly touched the bedspread, a combination of all three colors. It was the most beautiful room Libby had ever seen. She rubbed her hands down her shabby dress, feeling twice as shabby. How could Elizabeth Gail Dobbs stay in a room like this?

"Your suitcase is in the closet," said Mrs. Johnson. She picked up a fluffy pink dog off the bed. "Susan thought you might like this for your bed. She bought it as a welcoming gift."

Tears pricked Libby's eyes. She turned away and kept her back very stiff. She opened her eyes wide until the tears vanished.

"Sit down, Libby. I want to talk to you a minute." Mrs. Johnson sank down on the bed, the stuffed dog on her lap.

Libby sank slowly down onto a big, round red hassock. She kept her eyes glued to the brown plaid of her baggy dress.

"I am so glad you're going to live with us, Libby," said Mrs. Johnson softly. "You are our girl now. This is your home and we are your family. We do want you to like it here." Mrs. Johnson brushed a piece of pink fuzz off her black plaid pants, then leaned toward Libby. "Do you think you could . . . call me . . . Mom? I would like you to."

None of the others had wanted her to call them Mom. Libby shook her head no, wishing she could shout yes, yes. But why should she call this stranger Mom when she knew from past experience that she wouldn't be staying long?

"Calling me Mrs. Johnson is much too formal. My name is Vera. Call me that, and if you ever feel you can switch to calling me Mom, go ahead."

Libby nodded, her eyes smarting with unshed tears.

"I'll leave you alone for a while." She stood up to go. Libby could smell her perfume. It smelled even better than Miss Miller's. "I'll send Susan up after you later when Chuck gets home. He owns the general store in town and works until five every day except Sunday." Vera walked to the door, then turned back. "Welcome to our family, Libby. We're glad to have you." She shut the door softly.

Libby leaped up, looking wildly around. How could she stay here? Other homes she'd stayed in had been hard to leave, but this home would be impossible to leave! This was a dream home. A dream family. But Libby knew they'd be like all the other foster parents she'd had. As soon as they tired of her, they'd send her packing.

Libby closed her eyes and knotted her fists. How could she stand to be kicked out of this home? She could easily get to liking it here, liking the family. She shook her head violently, her braids bouncing. No! She couldn't allow it to happen.

With determined steps Libby walked toward the closet. It would be better to leave right now, now before she couldn't stand to leave. She jerked open the closet door and reached for her shabby suitcase. It wouldn't hurt so much this way.

THREE
Runaway

Stealthily Libby crept downstairs, her shabby suitcase clutched in her trembling hand. She didn't want to run away. She had to. This house, this family were too much for her. It was dangerous for her to stay another minute. If she stayed any longer it would hurt too much to leave. It would be too easy to love the family and the house.

Laughter floated up the steps, startling Libby. She clung to the well-polished railing. Her heart fluttered. Her hands were like ice.

Taking one quiet step at a time she finally reached the bottom of the stairs. Just ahead was the hall that led to the front door. Libby stood uncertainly in the hall doorway. The grandfather clock bonged five-thirty. Libby jumped. She wanted to dash out the door and down the long driveway to the road. But it was too cold to go without her jacket. Where was the room she'd hung it in? What way should she go?

Libby looked to her left. The room had a large stone fireplace at the far end with chairs and two couches arranged comfortably beside it. A round game table stood toward the middle of the room with heavy chairs around it, a game of Monopoly spread out on top. A piano stood against one wall and a large bookcase filled with books against another wall. A television set stood on the other side of the bookcase. Libby stared longingly at the piano. She closed her eyes, dreaming she was playing concert piano in front of a large audience. With a start she opened her eyes. Why dream such a foolish thing? She could never play the piano. She was only a foster child, an aid kid. Who would bother giving her lessons? How would she have the chance to take lessons?

Cautiously Libby looked to her right. The door to that room was closed. Which way to the back door? Another burst of laughter sent her flying. She carefully opened the heavy front door, stepped out into the cold, and closed the door. She shivered as the wind tugged at her dress. She'd have to walk around the house until she found the back door, go in, and get her jacket, and leave for good. She walked around the house, her heart in her mouth. If that goose chased her, she'd have to run back into the house. A stronger wind struck her as she turned the corner of the house. She shivered, hunching her thin shoulders. Finally she spotted the door. In relief she reached for the knob, then stopped. Where was the bell she'd rung earlier? She gasped, dropping her hand. It was the wrong door. Tears of frustration filled her eyes. Someone was bound to see her and stop her. That overly friendly goose would spot her and chase her and knock her down and maybe peck her eyes out.

Taking a deep breath, Libby hurried further around

the house until finally she found the right back door. She stepped inside, glad for the warmth. Quickly she grabbed her jacket and slipped it on. She shivered again. This time from excitement. She really didn't want to leave the Johnson family. Maybe someone would stop her and she wouldn't have to leave. Libby frowned. Nobody would dare stop her!

With one last look Libby hurried down the long driveway. She didn't look back. She didn't dare. Was anyone watching her leave? Would they care if she ran away?

The wind whipped her dress around her legs, chilling her to the bone.

At the end of the driveway she hesitated. She looked toward town. A big, colonial house stood about three hundred yards down the road on the top of a hill. She stood uncertainly, her suitcase bumping her leg. A dark green pickup drove into sight, slowed, and turned into the driveway beside Libby. Libby gasped, wondering wildly what she should do. Nervously she tried to hide her suitcase behind her.

The man in the pickup rolled down his window and stuck his bright red head out. He smiled. "Going somewhere, little lady? Can I give you a lift?"

Libby liked his smile. She liked his red hair. She wanted to smile and say something nice. Instead she stuck her pointed chin out and said defiantly, "I don't want to stay here. I'm going back to town."

"Hop in," the man said, opening the door.

For a minute Libby stood undecidedly, then dashed around and climbed into the warm pickup, her suitcase awkwardly hitting the seat.

"Why do you want to leave? You just got here." He

smiled again, making her feel warm all over. "You are Elizabeth Gail Dobbs, aren't you?"

She drew in her breath sharply. "Yes," she admitted reluctantly. How did he know?

"I'm Chuck Johnson."

Libby gasped. Her insides shriveled. "Are you taking me to town?" she asked defensively. How could this be happening to her?

"I'll take you for a little ride and we can talk," said Mr. Johnson, backing out of the drive and turning in the opposite direction from town.

Libby huddled against the door, the corners of her mouth drooping. Inside tears were falling. She locked her icy fingers together. Why couldn't she hate this man and his family? What was so special about them that made her like them already? She stared down at her hands and waited. She could smell the bunch of bananas on the seat between them.

"Now, Elizabeth, you tell me why you want to leave," said Mr. Johnson kindly.

No one had called her Elizabeth before. It sounded nice. It made her feel better. The inside tears stopped. "I want my own family," Libby said sharply. "Why should I have to stay with you?" Why couldn't she tell him the truth, that she was afraid of being hurt again?

"I can understand you wanting your own family, Elizabeth," said Mr. Johnson. He slowed the pickup and turned onto a dirt road. "Everyone does. But your parents aren't able to take care of you. And we want you in our family." He looked over at her, then back to the road. "We prayed about this for a long time. We asked God to send us just the right girl. He sent us you, Elizabeth."

Libby swallowed hard. They had prayed about her! She felt soft inside. Tears stung her eyelids.

"A long time ago when we first bought our farm," continued Mr. Johnson, "we dedicated it to God. We promised to use all 200 acres for him. In our house we have two spare bedrooms." He smiled at her again. "God gave you to us to fill the red room. He'll send us someone else for the other one." He was quiet for a long time. "We do want you. Give us a chance to make you happy. Give yourself a chance to make *us* happy."

She frowned. He was strange. How could she make anyone happy? She was a burden. She was only an aid kid. Nobody wanted her.

"God put a love for you in our hearts when we first heard your name and your case," said Mr. Johnson, turning to look at her again. She noticed he had hazel eyes like hers. "He gave you to us."

Libby couldn't keep the tears back a minute longer. They gushed down her thin, pale cheeks. She hadn't allowed herself to cry in front of anyone for a long, long time.

Mr. Johnson pushed a hanky into her hands. "Tears wash away a lot of pain and bad feelings. It's good for a person to cry, Elizabeth."

Finally Libby's tears stopped. She self-consciously wiped her eyes and blew her nose. She peeked at Mr. Johnson.

He smiled. "Good girl. Are you ready to go home?"

She nodded, almost smiling.

As they turned around, Mr. Johnson whistled a happy tune. Libby felt much better.

"I want you to remember one thing, Elizabeth," he said gently. "In our family each child is treated the same. You must obey, do your chores, and join in with family activities. We work together and we play together. We go to church every Sunday, sometimes more often. You will be expected to go with us without complaining." He grinned. "Don't let all this talk scare you. But I do think you'd feel better if I told you our rules, wouldn't you? It's much easier to get along when you know what's expected of you."

Libby listened thankfully as he continued to tell her more rules and some of the jobs she'd be expected to do. She relaxed against the back of the seat, determined to remember everything he told her.

He slowed to turn in the driveway of their farm. He looked at her and smiled. "Do you think you could call me Dad?"

She shrugged, her heart leaping with joy that he'd suggested it.

"If you can't, then call me Chuck until you get used to Dad."

A tiny smile touched her lips, then vanished. She looked at the house. It was more beautiful than before. Maybe if she tried harder, she could belong to this house and this family and they wouldn't send her away. He'd said God had given her to them. Maybe they were planning on keeping her. She clenched her fingers tighter. It wouldn't do to get her hopes up too much. They'd probably send her packing just the same as the other foster families she'd lived with.

FOUR
Sunday school

It was Sunday morning. Libby sat between Susan and Kevin in the backseat of the car as they rode to church. No more running away for her.

Libby touched the soft material on her new long-sleeved, blue-checked dress, then glanced down at her new black shoes. Church clothes. Beautiful clothes. She rubbed the long skirt over her thin legs. Never had she owned a long dress before. Vera had made it for her. Libby stole a quick look at Vera. Why hadn't she been able to tell Vera how much the dress meant to her? The least she could've done was to say thank you. Libby twisted her foot nervously.

Libby touched her hair. No longer was it long and straggly or braided in ugly braids. Vera had showed her a picture of a short, fluffy hairstyle and asked if she wouldn't like hers that way. Libby had agreed willingly.

"If you keep it clean and blow it dry it will always look soft and fluffy around your face," Vera had said after she finished cutting it and blowing it dry.

Libby had looked in the mirror and smiled in surprise. Her face didn't appear so thin nor her chin so pointed. Her hazel eyes were large and even pretty. Somehow she'd managed a smile for Vera and a very soft thank you.

Now, thought Libby in satisfaction, she didn't look like an aid kid. Maybe nobody would notice.

"I think you'll like our Sunday school class," said Susan cheerfully. She'd apologized to Libby for getting angry. If Libby would allow it, she and Susan would be friends.

"Connie is the best teacher in the world," continued Susan excitedly, her blue eyes sparkling. "Ben and I are in the same class. You'll meet all the other kids and make friends with all of them."

Libby clenched her hands in her lap. Her heart raced. Would all the kids in the class stare at her and make fun of her? Why should they? She was as well dressed as Susan. She was clean and she even smelled good. Susan had given her a tiny pink jar of cream sachet that smelled like roses.

"There are ten in our class most of the time," said Ben from the front seat. Libby liked to hear Ben talk. She liked to look at him, too. He really was good looking dressed in a long-sleeved blue plaid shirt, a dark blue sweater vest, and blue pants. He turned and smiled at her and she looked quickly down at her hands. Her heart beat faster.

"I'm in the younger junior boys' class," said Kevin, punching his glasses against his face, then rubbing his blond hair back. The silky hair slipped back over his forehead, almost touching the rim of his glasses. "Dad's my teacher."

"And he has to say I'm the best teacher in the world,"

said Chuck, grinning. He looked over his shoulder and winked at Libby.

"But you are the best, aren't you?" asked Vera, laughing. She squeezed Chuck's shoulder. "At least you're always telling us you're the best."

Libby enjoyed the way the family teased each other. They liked being together. She wanted to join in with the happiness and laughter, but she didn't know how. Inside she felt happy, mostly happy. She had to constantly remind herself that they had prayed for her to be in their family, that they really did want her. It was hard to believe, but Libby was trying.

Libby settled back against the soft back of the car seat as she thought how much she liked each evening with the family. After dinner they gathered in the family room around the fireplace for what they called family devotions. Vera would read a chapter out of a book, and Chuck would read out of the Bible. They would all sing for a while, and then pray. Libby had never seen anything like it.

As Chuck drove into the church parking lot, Libby looked around nervously. Several cars lined the double row of parking. People were walking into the church, some in the back and some the front. A bald-headed man waved at Chuck and he waved back.

Reluctantly Libby followed Susan up the sidewalk, shivering with cold as well as excitement. How she wished she were back in her beautiful bedroom, hugging Pinky.

Inside the warm classroom Susan introduced Libby to the boys and girls. Libby forgot all the names except Connie, the teacher, and Joe Wilkens, the boy who sat next to Ben.

"We're glad to have you in our class, Libby," said Connie, standing in front of the class, a Bible in her hands, a smile on her lips. Libby thought Connie's red dress was pretty with her dark hair and blue eyes. "Libby, we want you to be happy with us."

Libby could only nod. She wanted to smile and say she was glad to be there. She wanted Joe to think she was pretty.

As Connie took roll call and offering, Libby's mind drifted away to Miss Miller. Would Chuck report to Miss Miller that Libby had tried to run away? Would Vera tell her how much Susan and Libby fought? What if the report was so bad that Miss Miller placed Libby in another foster home?

Susan dug Libby in the ribs with her elbow. "Stop daydreaming," she whispered impatiently.

Libby frowned at Susan, then looked up as Connie placed bright-colored pictures on a flannel board and told about Joseph being sold into slavery. His brothers didn't want him. They were going to kill him, but they had a chance to sell him, so they did. Libby knew how Joseph felt. Nobody wanted her either. Except maybe the Johnsons. Libby locked her fingers together and forced back tears of sympathy for Joseph.

Although she'd never heard it before, she knew the story was from the Bible. During the past five years, going from one foster home to another, she had attended church only the three months she lived with the Swansons. It hadn't been fun sitting quietly beside them as they pretended to listen to the big words the man in the black robe spoke.

After Connie dismissed the class in prayer she reminded them about the party she was having for them at her house Friday night. "Come about seven-thirty," she said, smiling right into Libby's eyes. Libby felt warm all over. She wanted to smile back. She looked over at Ben just as he looked at her. Ben smiled. Libby tried, but couldn't. She looked at Joe Wilkens. He smiled. She looked quickly away, locking and unlocking her fingers.

"The party will be fun," said Susan as she stood up. Impatiently she tugged at Libby's arm. "We have to go sit in church now."

Libby walked hesitantly beside Susan through the door that led into the sanctuary. She'd rather have stayed in class to listen to Connie tell another Bible story.

"Connie always has fun parties," said Susan.

"Are you going to the party, Libby?" asked Joe from behind her.

A tingle ran down to her toes. She shrugged. "I don't know if I want to." She wanted to bite her tongue off for answering like that.

"She's going," said Ben. "We all three are."

"Me too," said Joe, sliding into the pew three rows from the front.

Ben slid in beside him. Susan nudged Libby in closer to Ben, then Susan sat beside Libby. Ben smiled at Libby and she was finally able to make the corners of her mouth turn up just a little. Her hazel eyes sparkled. She liked Ben. He was teaching her to ride during the afternoons just after school. Libby was slowly learning. Ben didn't get impatient with her like Susan always did.

The young teen class filed into the church. Libby watched as a dark-haired, dark-eyed girl dressed in orange and brown pushed past two girls and walked to the pew where Libby was sitting. The girl shoved past Susan and Libby.

"Move over. I want to sit with Ben," she whispered, bumping her knees against the sides of Libby's legs.

"I want to sit here," whispered Libby, daring the girl to push in between Ben and her.

"I always sit with Ben," hissed the girl, her dark eyes angry.

"Not today," said Libby, moving nearer Ben.

"Sit somewhere else, Brenda," said Ben softly.

The girl pushed hard against Libby's legs, crushing them against the side of the pew.

Libby pinched the soft skin on the girl's leg just above the knee. The girl screamed, causing everyone to look at her.

"I'll get you for this, aid kid," hissed the girl. "Now, move over, aid kid."

"You'd better, Libby," said Susan, sliding down to make room for Libby to move.

All the joy seeped out of Libby. The happiness vanished as she slid over next to Susan. Hot tears stung Libby's eyelids as the rude girl plopped down beside Ben. That terrible, terrible girl had called her an aid kid. Susan and Ben had heard. Joe had heard. Maybe others, too. Her new dress and shoes and hairdo didn't make any difference. She was an aid kid. Nothing more.

FIVE
Snowball's accident

"You should have heard her, Mom," said Susan disgustedly as they drove home after church. "Brenda Wilkens is terrible."

"Now, Susan," said Vera, frowning. "Be careful of what you say."

"She's always terrible," said Kevin, turning around in the front seat and making a face.

"Kevin," warned Chuck.

Libby sat staring out the window. So, Brenda Wilkens was that awful girl's name. Probably Joe's sister.

A dog ran out from a farmyard, barking at the wheels of the car, startling Libby.

"That crazy dog is going to get run over yet," said Ben, leaning toward the window to watch the dog.

Libby shrank from Ben's touch. She didn't want anyone touching her or looking at her or talking to her.

"I hope Brenda doesn't butt in on our party at Connie's house Friday," said Susan, thumping her Bible on her knee.

"She won't," said Ben, settling back in his seat. "She knows she's too old."

"She's not too old to like you," said Susan. "She doesn't care that you're twelve and she's thirteen."

"I'll be thirteen next month," said Ben gruffly.

"When's your birthday, Libby?" asked Kevin, peering around from the front.

Libby kept her face turned to the window.

"Libby," persisted Kevin. "When's your birthday?"

"It's none of your business," snapped Libby. What did she care about this family? She was an aid kid and she didn't belong to them.

"Libby," said Vera reproachfully. "Answer him right."

"Remember our talk, Elizabeth," said Chuck, glancing quickly over his shoulder, then back to the road.

"February 14th," said Libby in a low voice.

"Valentine's Day!" exclaimed Kevin, grinning. "You're a real sweetheart then."

Everyone laughed except Libby. Here was just one more thing to be teased about. She couldn't stop Kevin's teasing now, but just wait until she was alone with him!

"What is wrong with Brenda Wilkens?" asked Susan, going back to her first gripe. She pushed her long, red-gold hair over her shoulder. "I can't understand that girl."

"She's not a Christian for one thing," said Chuck as he slowed for a curve. "Brenda and Joe haven't been in church very often."

"We're thankful Brenda and Joe are going regularly to church now," said Vera, looking back at Susan.

"Ben is the only reason Brenda comes," said Susan.

"It is not," said Ben, poking Susan hard in the ribs

with his elbow. "She likes coming. So does Joe."

"See that house, Libby?" said Kevin, pointing to the large colonial house sitting on a hill. "That's where the Wilkenses live. Almost across from us."

Libby groaned. Having Brenda Wilkens that close would be terrible!

Chuck drove into the driveway, past the tall trees and into the garage. Goosy Poosy honked and came running.

Libby cringed behind Kevin so the goose wouldn't touch her. She had made friends with the big collie Rex and the assortment of cats, and of course the horses, but she was still afraid of Goosy Poosy.

"Get some grain for him," said Chuck as he rubbed the goose's long white neck. "How are you today, friend? You look very pretty dressed in your Sunday feathers."

"Here's the grain," said Ben, setting down a container of feed for the goose.

Libby sighed with relief as the goose's attention was diverted for a while. Carefully holding up her long dress, she hurried inside.

"Girls, hurry and change your clothes so you can help with dinner," said Vera as she hurried to the kitchen to check on the chicken in the oven.

Libby sniffed, closing her eyes and holding her stomach. Chicken was her favorite.

"When I talk to that Brenda Wilkens next, I'll make her apologize for calling you an aid kid," said Susan as she walked beside Libby up the carpeted stairs.

Libby felt better. "You don't need to say anything to her, Sue."

Susan swished her green skirt. "I'm going to. You

can count on it. She'll never say anything mean to you again."

Tears pricked Libby's eyelids. Susan was actually standing up for her. Libby wanted to tell Susan how good it made her feel, but the words wouldn't come.

"I think Joe likes you," continued Susan as they stopped outside Libby's door. "He's nice. But Brenda!"

Libby flushed and ducked her head as she hurried into her room. She picked up the pink dog and hugged him. "I love you, Pinky," she whispered. "I liked Sunday school too until that bad girl called me an aid kid. Her name's Brenda Wilkens and I hate her." Libby sank down on the red hassock with Pinky on her lap. "But I like Joe. Susan says he likes me. Do you think so, Pinky?"

Libby jumped up, kissed Pinky on his black nose, and dropped him back onto the bed. She pulled off her long dress and carefully hung it in the closet. She slipped on a pair of jeans that Vera had bought her and an orange sweater. She pulled on her new blue sneakers. It felt so good to wear clothes that fit and looked good on her. Quickly she brushed her hair, making a face at her reflection in the wide mirror over her dresser.

"Ready?" asked Susan, poking her head around the door.

"Sure," said Libby. She thought Susan looked pretty in her red and blue jeans and her red blouse. She'd fixed her red-gold hair in two pony tails that hung over each ear.

"Shall we finish that game of Monopoly that we started last night?" asked Susan as they hurried together downstairs.

"OK," said Libby with satisfaction. So far she owned more property than either Susan or Ben. Maybe this time she'd win.

"I'm starved," said Susan, jumping down off the last three steps.

"Me too," said Libby, grinning at the way Susan's pony tails flipped around. Libby's stomach growled as she sniffed dinner.

Vera broke off in the middle of a song to tell the girls to set the table, then continued singing as the girls hurried to work. Libby liked to hear Vera sing.

"If you can stop the melody and tell me what to do, I'll help," said Chuck as he hugged Vera and kissed her behind the ear.

She turned around in his arms and kissed him. "You can make the salad."

He kissed her again. "If you'll stop hanging onto me, I'll toss the salad," he said, laughing.

A lump filled Libby's throat. Chuck and Vera were happy together. Why hadn't Mother and Dad stayed together and been happy?

"Dad! Dad! Come quick!" cried Kevin, puffing as he dashed into the dining room.

Libby's hand flew to her throat.

"What is it son?" asked Chuck, clamping his hand over Kevin's shoulder.

"It's Snowball. She got her leg tangled in some barbed wire."

Libby gasped. She remembered a piece of barbed wire lying in the pen that she was supposed to throw into the dump. She'd forgotten to do it.

"Is it bad?" asked Chuck as he hurried out with Kevin.

"Real bad." Kevin's answer floated back before the door slammed.

Libby turned away, sagging against a chair.

"You forgot to throw that wire away, Libby," cried Susan, her hands on her hips. "How could you forget?"

"Leave me alone!" shouted Libby, her fists doubled at her sides, her back stiff.

"Girls! We'll go see how bad it is," said Vera, drying her hands.

A heavy hand seemed to squeeze Libby's heart. Now she just knew she'd have to leave the Johnson family.

"Come, Libby," said Vera gently but firmly, taking Libby's cold hand and nodding to Susan to follow.

Libby couldn't stand to think of Snowball suffering. In just the few days she'd been here she'd learned to love the little filly. Libby hung back, but Vera tugged her on.

The wind was cold even through her heavy jacket as Libby ran beside Vera and Susan to the horse barn. Goosy Poosy honked and followed them. Libby didn't notice. All she could think about was Snowball.

"How is it?" asked Vera as they stepped inside the protection of the barn.

"Not as bad as it looked," said Chuck, cleaning off the bloody leg.

Ben's arms were wrapped around the filly's neck as Chuck worked on the back left leg.

A sour taste filled Libby's mouth. She was going to be sick. Weakly she leaned against the stall, her head down. Pungent barn odors filled her nostrils. A gray cat rubbed around her legs, purring happily.

"Will we have to call the vet?" asked Vera, frowning in concern as she watched Chuck.

"I don't think so," he answered, first looking up and then back down at Snowball's leg. "She had a tetanus shot just last week. We'll watch the leg closely, and if it isn't better by the middle of the week, we'll call the vet."

Libby groaned and pressed her forehead against the rough wood.

"It'll be all right, Elizabeth," said Chuck. "We'll keep salve on it and keep it wrapped a few days. Do you think you could be in charge of it?"

"Her?" cried Ben. "But . . . Dad!"

Chuck looked sharply at Ben and frowned. "You can help her, Ben."

Libby slowly stood up. "I'll take care of Snowball's leg. I . . . I didn't mean for her to get hurt. I . . . forgot to throw away the barbed wire."

"We'll talk about it later," said Chuck as he reached for the salve. "Ben, stay and help me. The rest of you go to the house."

Susan and Kevin glared at Libby, then ran past her to the house.

"Could I stay and help?" asked Libby in a very squeaky voice.

Chuck studied her searchingly, then nodded. "Ben, go with Mom to the house."

Ben wouldn't look at Libby as he walked past her.

"Come in as soon as you can," said Vera, squeezing Libby's arm affectionately.

Libby stared down at her feet. She'd managed to spoil the whole day for everyone.

"Hold Snowball while I rub this salve on," said Chuck. He had blood on his jacket sleeve. The salve smelled terrible. Libby's nose burned from smelling it.

She held Snowball firmly, determined to do a good job even though the smell made her sick. The fuzzy filly was warm in her arms.

Finally Chuck stood up, rubbing his back. He gathered up his kit and put it away in the tack room. Libby followed with a heavy heart. What would he say to her? Would he warn her and let it go at that? Or would he tell her she'd have to leave?

Chuck put his arm around Libby's shoulders as they walked slowly from the barn. The cold wind whipped against them. The sky was gray with just a weak sun trying to shine. Goosy Poosy honked and ran to them. Libby jumped behind Chuck away from the goose. Her heart raced.

"Go find your grain, Goosy Poosy," commanded Chuck with a laugh.

"Snowball's leg could have been hurt even worse," said Chuck, putting his arm around Libby again. She kept her eyes on the grass they were walking on. "Because you didn't do your work when you were told, you forgot all about it. It didn't hurt you, but it did hurt Snowball. Leaving the barbed wire in the pen probably seemed like a very small thing to you since you haven't lived on a farm before. But as you can see now, it wasn't a small matter. I want you to remember from now on to do your work when you're told to do it. Understand?"

"Yes," she whispered, tears stinging her eyes, a lump filling her throat. He hadn't said she'd have to leave if she didn't remember. Was that what he meant?

"Vera and I pray for you, Elizabeth. We want you to grow into a fine, happy girl. We want Christ to be the center of your life."

Libby opened the back door and hung up her coat. She didn't know what to say.

He put his hands on her shoulders and turned her around to face him. "I have something special planned for this afternoon. Would you like to know what it is?"

Libby stiffened. Slowly she nodded.

"I'm going to hitch up Jack and Dan and we're going to take a ride in the wagon to see how Ben's Christmas trees are. We'll show you our farm."

Excitement bubbled up inside Libby. She'd finally get to ride in the wagon with the big gray horses pulling it. Her eyes sparkled as she and Chuck hurried to get washed for dinner.

SIX
Wagon ride

"Let's call Joe and Brenda to see if they want to go on the wagon ride with us," said Ben as they finished washing and drying dinner dishes. "They'd love to go."

Libby didn't want Brenda Wilkens going on any ride where she was. Was Ben suggesting it just because he was still mad about Snowball's leg? He'd been nice to her all through dinner. Had he been nice only because his parents were present?

"It would be nice to invite them," said Vera, rubbing hand cream into her hands. "I know they don't go many places with their parents."

"Not this time," said Chuck, sliding an arm around Libby. "We want to show our girl the farm with just the family."

Libby looked up at him, her eyes sparkling. She wanted to tell him thank you, but she couldn't make the words come out.

"Come on, Libby," said Susan excitedly. "We've got to put on our insulated underwear and warm coats so we don't freeze. It's really cold riding in the wagon." Her red-gold pony tails bobbed with each bounce of enthusiasm.

Libby followed Susan, thinking that as warm as she felt right now, she'd not even need a coat. Susan had completely forgotten to be angry about Snowball. Libby watched apprehensively to see if Susan would drop the friendly act the minute they were alone. She didn't. She continued being nice. Libby relaxed and enjoyed her friendliness even though she didn't understand Susan at all. Why wasn't Susan thinking of mean things to do to Libby to get back at her for hurting Snowball?

Later, with flushed cheeks, Libby climbed into the wagon and sat on the backseat between Ben and Susan. Kevin sat on the front seat with Chuck and Vera. Vera adjusted her bright red scarf so that it hung down her back. Her blonde hair was completely covered.

Apprehensively Libby looked down at the ground. It seemed a long way down. Goosy Poosy honked, rubbing his neck on the big round wagon wheels. Rex stood ready beside Dan. Jack nickered, shaking his harness.

Libby held her breath as the wagon started with a creak, swaying enough to make Libby nervous. She lurched forward, then grabbed the wooden seat and held on so tightly her knuckles ached. Finally she realized she could balance herself and she relaxed and enjoyed the swaying wagon ride.

With Ben on one side and Susan on the other Libby felt warm and protected. Ben pointed out the pond where they would go ice skating as soon as the ice was thick enough. Susan excitedly showed her where they came for picnics. They rode through the cattle pasture. Ben opened and closed the gates. Libby almost screamed when a cow stopped right in front of the team of horses and mooed to them.

Chuck kept on going and the cow moved just in time.

Libby saw more trees than she'd ever seen in her life. Kevin pointed out a red squirrel next to a tall poplar.

The wagon creaked up a hill, causing Libby to hang on again. She was sure she was going to slide off the seat and land on the ground. They rode across a large hayfield and into the large grove of Christmas trees.

"Dad and I planted the big blue spruce when I was four years old. Each year after that I'd plant a new section of trees," explained Ben, his blue eyes sparkling with pleasure and pride. "Different people like different sizes."

"Kevin and I helped plant those," said Susan, pointing to tiny trees poking from the ground. "We put in five hundred blue spruce two years ago and five hundred this year."

It would be so much fun to ride out here and choose a Christmas tree. As Chuck drove the team to the far side of the trees Libby pretended she was the customer choosing a Christmas tree for her family. Finally she spotted a tall, heavily branched tree. She closed her eyes and pictured it standing in front of the living room window, decorated with ornaments, tinsel, blinking lights, and candy canes all over it. She opened her eyes when the wagon stopped.

"We'll get out and stretch our legs a while," said Chuck, leaping from the wagon, then helping Vera jump down.

Libby waited until Susan and Ben were out before

she carefully jumped from the wagon. Her legs were rubbery. She leaned against the wagon, hoping nobody had noticed that she'd almost fallen.

"I can hardly wait until the Christmas season," said Ben as they walked slowly from tree to tree.

"Wait a minute, Ben," said Vera, laughing gaily. "What about Thanksgiving? We don't want my fine turkey to go to waste, do we?"

"Grandma and Grandpa are coming for Thanksgiving," said Kevin to Libby.

Libby swallowed hard. She didn't know if she wanted to meet them. What if they didn't like her because she was an aid kid?

Kevin grabbed Libby's hand and looked up at her with twinkling eyes behind his glasses. "You're going to be our surprise to them. We're going to pop you out at them and say, 'We have a new girl in our family. Her name is Elizabeth Gail Dobbs.' They'll be so surprised." Kevin laughed in delight.

Libby's heart zoomed to her feet. Surprises didn't always work out the way people hoped they would.

"You will like them, Libby," said Ben softly. "And they'll like you."

Libby wanted to tell him thank you for the kind words, but she couldn't talk around the lump in her throat.

"Everybody back in the wagon," said Chuck.

Libby climbed in and took the same spot in between Susan and Ben. She sat straight and pretended she wasn't a bit upset about meeting more of the Johnson family.

"Look, Libby," said Susan excitedly, pointing to a

small Christmas tree. "See those two red birds? They're cardinals."

The birds were beautiful. Libby wanted to look at them longer, but the movement of the wagon and horses startled them and they flew away.

Libby laid her mittened hands in her lap and forced herself to forget about meeting the grandparents so she could enjoy the rest of the wagon ride.

SEVEN
Punch in the nose

"Snowball's leg sure is better," said Ben on Tuesday as he held the filly while Libby applied the salve.

"I'm glad," said Libby, screwing the lid on the jar of thick yellow medicine. She put her arms around Snowball's neck and kissed her between the eyes. "I love you," she mouthed so Ben couldn't hear.

"Are you ready for today's riding lesson?" he asked as they walked to the tack room.

Libby put the salve in the big chest and closed the lid. "I've got to change my jeans first. I got them wet watering the sheep."

"Hurry back," said Ben, lifting down a saddle as Libby raced away.

"Kevin, I'm ready to go in," called Libby as she stopped just outside the barn door. Apprehensively she looked around for Goosy Poosy. He was swaying along beside Kevin near the chicken house.

"I'll keep Goosy Poosy beside me while you run to the house," yelled Kevin. He knelt beside the goose and wrapped his arms firmly around him.

Libby flipped her hood over her head and raced for the house, listening for any sounds that the goose was following her. Breathlessly she opened the back door and jumped inside. Her cheeks were flushed red. Her lips were blue from the cold. Quickly she pulled off her jacket and hung it haphazardly on the hook beside the red plaid coat.

Susan stopped her as she dashed through the family room toward the stairs. "Libby, tell me how to do this math, will you? I'm having so much trouble with it, and you know how crabby Mr. Spenser gets if I don't hand my paper in on time."

"I'm on my way to change my jeans," said Libby, breathing hard. "Ben's saddling up for my riding lesson."

"He won't mind waiting," said Susan, biting the red eraser on her yellow pencil. "Please."

Libby shrugged and hurried to Susan's side. Patiently she explained how to work the math. "If you have any more trouble, I'll help you when I get back."

"Thanks, Libby." Susan smiled her appreciation before she bent her red-gold head over her work.

A warm feeling spread over Libby as she hurried to change. She liked helping Susan as long as Susan didn't get impatient with her. Mostly she did. But not Ben. Libby smiled as she zipped her jeans, glad that it was time to go riding with Ben.

Excitedly she hurried out of the house, looked around for Goosy Poosy, then dashed to the horse barn. She stopped short as Ben came out with Brenda and Joe Wilkens beside him.

"Hi, Libby," greeted Joe with a big smile. "We're going riding with you."

Libby wanted to dash back to the house. She looked questioningly at Ben. Didn't he know how she felt? She couldn't ride with the others watching. She wasn't that good yet.

"Apache Girl's saddled for you," said Ben, leading the way to where four horses were saddled and waiting.

"I don't want to go," she whispered in agony to Ben. She could feel Brenda's eyes boring into her back.

"Of course you do," said Ben as he slipped the reins loose from the fence.

"Ride with me, Ben," said Brenda, standing close to Ben. "Joe can ride with . . . with . . ."

"Libby," said Joe, frowning at his sister. He turned to Libby with a smile. "Come on. I'll help you. Ben says you're learning fast."

"I . . . I don't think I want to go," said Libby barely above a whisper.

"I want you to," said Joe. "Besides, I don't want to ride near my sister. And I sure don't want to ride alone."

Libby stood hesitantly beside Apache Girl, then reluctantly allowed Joe to help her mount. She clutched the saddle horn, experiencing again the feeling of being twenty feet off the ground. She watched in dismay as Ben and Brenda rode off together down the trail, leaving her behind with Joe. How could Ben leave her when he knew how much help she needed? She frowned, almost in frustrated tears. What if Apache Girl ran away with her?

"Relax a little, Libby, and you'll ride easier," suggested Joe. "I've been riding four years now, so you can trust me to help you."

A chilly wind blew against Libby's face. The sky turned gray. Her hands were icy cold even through her gloves. Reluctantly she rode along beside Joe, gradually relaxing under his friendly attitude.

They rode until every muscle she had ached. Finally they rode back to the yard.

"Ben and Brenda are back already," said Joe.

Libby watched as Brenda stayed close beside Ben while he unsaddled both horses. Ben laughed at something Brenda said. Libby frowned. What could Brenda say that was funny? Libby didn't want to ride into the yard with Brenda there, but she knew she had to.

"We wondered if you two were coming back," said Brenda as they stopped their horses beside the board fence Brenda was leaning against.

"Why wouldn't we come back?" asked Joe impatiently as he slid off his horse.

Libby bit her lower lip, determined not to say a word to Brenda. Libby just wanted to climb down and limp to the house. Slowly, awkwardly Libby slid off Apache Girl beside Ben. Her legs buckled. Ben steadied her with a grin.

"You'll be all right in a minute," he said, holding her.

"Can't you ever leave Ben alone?" asked Brenda, shoving against Libby. "Must you always hang onto him?"

Libby's head snapped up. "I can hang onto him if I want."

"Leave Ben alone," cried Brenda, her hands on her hips, her dark eyes blazing.

"Be quiet, Brenda," said Joe angrily.

"You'll be lucky to last here a month," hissed Brenda, her face close to Libby.

Libby clenched her fists at her side. Ben stood uneasily beside her.

"Let's go home, Brenda," said Joe, taking her arm.

She jerked away from him, flipping her hair over her shoulder. "I want to stay."

Libby wanted to yank Brenda's hair off her head. Instead she turned and lifted Ben's saddle off the fence and carried it to the tack room. Ben could unsaddle Apache Girl and take care of her. Libby would do her share of work and then rush to the house to get away from Brenda. She didn't want to see that terrible girl again.

Awkwardly Libby put the heavy saddle in place in the tack room. She turned to leave, but the others came with saddles and blocked her way. Impatiently she stepped aside and finally was able to go back outdoors. A bridle lay on the ground near the horses. Libby sighed. She had to take care of it. Slowly she picked it up and carried it inside, her teeth clenched tightly, determined she wouldn't say anything even if Brenda said something ugly to her.

Together the four walked out of the barn, Libby next to Joe.

Without a word Libby started for the house. Goosy Poosy honked and came running, neck out, toward Libby. She screamed and ran back to Ben, hiding behind him, her hands tight around his arms. With wildly beating heart she peeked around Ben.

"Are you afraid of that goose?" asked Brenda with a sneer.

Libby ignored her as she kept Ben between herself and the goose.

Joe grabbed a handful of grain and called the goose.

Goosy Poosy honked and quickly waddled over to Joe.

Libby relaxed her grip on Ben's arms. Her heart settled back in place.

"You're just pretending to be afraid of that dumb goose," said Brenda, grabbing Libby's arm. "Stop it! And stay away from Ben!"

Libby jerked away from Brenda, glaring at her.

"You don't belong here," hissed Brenda. "You're nothing but an aid kid."

Libby's fist shot out, striking Brenda square on the nose.

Brenda screamed and covered her nose, blood streaming down through her fingers.

Libby stared wide-eyed at Ben, fearing he'd run and tell on her. She gasped. Ben was doubled over with laughter, with Joe right beside him, also laughing until tears streamed down his cheeks. The corners of Libby's mouth came up; laughter filled her throat and burst out.

"Stop it," screamed Brenda. "Stop laughing!"

"You . . . you got . . . just what . . . you . . . deserved," said Joe in between laughs. "Here, take this hanky. Let's go home and clean you up." Joe grabbed her arm and pulled her down the driveway.

Libby wiped her eyes as the laughter died away.

Ben slapped her on the back. "That's the funniest thing I've ever seen, Libby. I'll remember never to make you mad at me." He laughed again and finally Libby joined in.

EIGHT
Mystery of the open gate

The rest of Tuesday Libby waited for Mrs. Wilkens to call Vera about Brenda's bloody nose. The call didn't come. Wednesday in school Libby saw Brenda only once, but she made sure Brenda didn't see her.

By suppertime Libby began to relax. Ben grinned at her knowingly as he passed a plate of hamburger patties. Libby forked a hamburger and handed the plate to Vera.

"How are you doing in math, Susan?" asked Chuck, setting down his cup of tea.

Susan shrugged, but smiled thankfully at Libby. "A lot better, Dad. Libby's been helping me. She's better in math and science than I am."

Libby swelled with pride at Susan's praise.

"Maybe you'll be a scientist when you grow up, Elizabeth," said Chuck with a wink.

Libby listened as the table talk continued about what each one was going to be when he or she grew up. Libby wouldn't tell them of her dreams to be a concert pianist or a horse trainer.

The phone rang as the family started on the chocolate pudding covered with whipping cream.

Libby dropped her spoon. Ben choked on a bite. Chuck answered the phone in the kitchen.

His voice could be heard from the kitchen—the surprise in it, not the actual words. Libby waited with a sinking heart. She kept her eyes on her pudding. She looked up when Chuck slowly walked back in. His face was flushed, his hair mussed from his running his fingers through it.

"The sheep are out. They're in the Wilkenses' winter wheat." Chuck's eyes bored into Libby's. "You are in charge of the sheep, Elizabeth. Did you close and lock the gate securely?"

She nodded yes, a lump lodged in her throat. She remembered distinctly closing and locking the gate after she'd fed and watered the sheep. Ice settled around her heart as she realized Chuck didn't believe her.

"Libby," he said. She cringed. He never called her Libby. He seemed to know she liked being called Elizabeth. "Libby, you didn't lie about leaving the barbed wire out when Snowball got caught in it. Why lie now?"

"I didn't leave it open," whispered Libby, her icy hands on the edge of the table.

The silence in the room made her want to scream.

"Libby," warned Vera. "It is better to tell the truth."

"You're the only one that did the sheep chores," said Ben.

"I'll handle this, Ben," said Chuck. "Libby, the truth please."

She shoved her chair back so hard it fell over. Angry tears filled her eyes. "I didn't leave it open. You can't make me say I did!"

"Libby!" exclaimed Vera. "Go to your room. I've warned you about speaking in that tone of voice. We'll talk about it later."

Libby rushed to the door, then turned back. "I did not leave that gate open!" She raced from the room, into the front hall, and up the stairs. She knew she hadn't left the gate open. She had been very, very careful. She'd taken care of the sheep last of all and she'd closed the gate and locked it the same as always.

Chuck was very angry with her. Now he'd send her back to find another foster home. She'd have more strangers to live with.

Libby flung herself across the beautiful bed, hugging Pinky and sobbing into his fluffy fur. Why had she stayed here with the Johnsons? She knew something like this would happen to cause her to leave. Her next home would probably be in the city again. She'd never see Snowball or ride Apache Girl or even be chased by that dumb Goosy Poosy.

Finally Libby pushed herself up and sat dejectedly on the edge of the bed. She rubbed her red-rimmed eyes. What could she say to make Chuck believe her? It was only her word that she hadn't left the gate open. No one had ever taken her word about anything before. Why should the family believe her now?

Listlessly Libby walked to the window, looking out over the back of the farm. It was still light enough to make out the big collie running through the yard. His barks barely reached her ears. Had Chuck and Ben been able to get all the sheep in? Libby pressed her fists against her cheeks. Why didn't anything ever go right for her?

Slowly she walked to her dresser, picked up her

brush and laid it back down. She opened the jar of cream sachet and closed it again. Who had left the gate open? A sheep couldn't have nudged it open. Who did it? Ben? Susan? Kevin? No! They would speak up if they had. None of them ever lied.

Libby grabbed her hair with both hands and pulled until it hurt. She didn't lie either! Chuck and Vera just had to believe her. How could she change their minds?

In a daze she sank down on the big red hassock, her chin in her hands. Libby leaped up as Chuck and Vera walked in.

"The sheep are all in. They didn't do any damage," said Chuck tiredly.

"A lie is a terrible thing," said Vera. She blew her nose and wiped her eyes. "Please, Libby, won't you tell us the truth?"

Libby closed her eyes tight and sank down on the hassock. Should she say she'd left the gate open? Was that what they wanted?

"The gate didn't open by itself, Elizabeth," said Chuck. "Tell me what happened."

She looked up at them tiredly. "I didn't leave it open," she said barely above a whisper. "Do you want me to say I did?"

Chuck slid his arm around Vera and pulled her down beside him on the edge of Libby's bed. His red hair blended in with the room.

"You haven't lived with us very long, Elizabeth," said Chuck slowly. "I don't believe you've lied to us yet." He was quiet a long time. "I do want to believe you."

"It must have been an accident," said Vera, knotting the hanky in her hand. "You probably thought you locked it securely."

Libby's heart sank. She had locked it securely.

"That's the only answer," said Chuck, nodding. "We're sorry for upsetting you so much. Be very careful from now on. If the sheep get out again, they can do a lot of damage."

Pain squeezed Libby's heart. She hadn't left it open even accidentally, but she wouldn't say another word about it. At least they weren't sending her away. Not this time.

NINE
Connie's party

Libby shivered and hung back as Susan and Ben walked up to Connie's house. Libby thought about how friendly Connie had been in Sunday school and what good stories she told, but still Libby was reluctant to join in with all the class for the party.

"Come on, Libby," said Susan impatiently. "It's too cold out here. Hurry up."

Libby hurried. Were her green pants and green checked pullover all right? Did she look like a long stringbean? Would the other kids make fun of her because she was an aid kid?

"Come in," called Connie gaily as she opened the door. "Come right in and put your coats in the bedroom. Libby, I'm so glad you came. We are all anxious to get to know you better."

Libby ducked her head and twisted her toe in the thick carpet.

"The others are in the basement," continued Connie. "As soon as you take off your coats, then join them. I'll be down as soon as everyone's here."

Susan flung her coat on the heap of coats on the bed. "I wonder if Joe's coming."

"I guess so," said Ben, combing his hair.

"Brenda too?" asked Susan, making a face.

Ben shrugged that he didn't know.

Libby's heart zoomed to her feet. Brenda wouldn't come, would she? She was too old to be in Connie's Sunday school class. She just couldn't come and ruin Libby's chance to have a good time! Libby laid her coat on top of Ben's. She wanted the evening to be fun. She'd almost had to stay home as a punishment. Someone had cut the bell rope off and Libby, of course, had been blamed. She'd almost convinced them she hadn't done it when she'd discovered the rope stuffed in her coat pocket. Finally Chuck had convinced himself and Vera that Libby had accidentally broken off the rope but was too afraid to own up to it. Libby had stood silently, tired of arguing a losing fight, knowing full well the rope had been cut on purpose and put in her pocket to make her appear guilty. Who could've done it?

Libby watched Susan brush her hair in front of Connie's mirror. Had Susan cut off the rope and hid it in Libby's pocket because Libby had beat Susan twice in a row at Monopoly? Had Kevin done it because she'd slapped him for teasing her again about being a Valentine sweetheart?

"Hurry, Susan," said Ben impatiently. "Your hair is OK."

Brenda and Joe walked in before they could leave. Libby tried to make herself invisible. Joe smiled at her. Brenda stared right at her. Libby could see the hatred in the girl's eyes.

"Let's go to the basement," said Susan, nudging Libby.

Libby wanted to grab her coat and leave, but she followed Susan.

"I'm coming too," said Ben. He leaned close to Libby's ear. "Keep your temper tonight. We don't want to ruin Connie's party."

Libby agreed silently. She was already in enough trouble without adding anything else to the long list.

"Ben! Wait for me," called Brenda, rushing after them and grabbing Ben's arm.

Libby gritted her teeth.

"Wouldn't you know it?" whispered Susan in Libby's ear. "*She* had to come."

The basement seemed full of kids to Libby. She stayed close to Susan as they walked past the Ping-Pong table. A fireplace stood at the far corner, burning brightly. Comfortable couches and chairs were arranged near it. Three kids were sitting on the floor in front of the fire. A piano stood against one wall and a snack bar against another.

"I see a game of Careers," said Susan, grabbing Libby's arm. "Let's play that."

"I'll play," said Ben.

"Me too," said Brenda, sticking right close to Ben.

Libby clenched her fists. She didn't want to play any game with Brenda.

"I'm going to play darts over there," said Joe, smiling at Libby. "Want to, Libby?"

Libby nodded thankfully as she followed Joe across to the dart board. Joe looked nice in his blue jeans and long-sleeved blue plaid shirt.

"Ben and I decided ahead of time to keep you and Brenda apart if she came," whispered Joe, grinning. "We don't want another bloody nose."

Libby giggled. "Thanks, Joe."

"Do you know how to play darts?" he asked as he pulled the darts from the board.

"Sure," said Libby, remembering when she was nine and the family she'd lived with liked playing darts. They'd allowed her to play only when they weren't.

Libby won one game and Joe two before Connie came downstairs and called them all together for planned games.

"Divide into two teams," said Connie, holding two fingers up to stress the point. "Dave, you be the captain for team one and Meg, team two."

Libby wanted to sink through the floor. She just knew she wouldn't be chosen. To Libby's surprise Meg picked her on the third call. Dave called Brenda the fourth call. She glared at Libby as she took her place almost opposite Libby. She turned her head, determined to ignore Brenda. During the evening of games Libby tried her best to be polite.

Finally the group sat down, with Connie in front of them, lifting her hand for silence.

"We've had a lot of fun tonight, kids. While we're resting, let's sing some songs." She sat at the piano and started a chorus that Libby had heard them sing in church.

Libby looked around the group of happy faces. Most of them were singing joyfully. Libby couldn't. She didn't know the songs, but it was peaceful to sit and listen. She sat crosslegged on the floor in between

Susan and Joe, thinking how nice it would be to join in.

Finally Connie twisted around on the bench. She smiled, her blue eyes sparkling. "Now, kids, I've typed Scripture verses on pieces of orange paper and hid them about the basement. I want each of you to find one paper and then come sit down again."

Libby looked quickly around the room. She couldn't see even a hint of orange paper.

"One, two three, go!" said Connie. She turned back to the piano and played a lively march as the kids scurried around the room.

After several kids found their papers and sat down, Libby began to feel desperate. She couldn't stand to be the last person to find a paper. It would be too embarrassing to have everyone looking at her, thinking how dumb she was not to find her paper.

Finally Libby spotted an orange paper hidden between the cushions of the easy chair near the fireplace. Excitedly she took out the paper. Brenda grabbed it from her.

"I saw it first," she whispered fiercely.

Libby grabbed for the paper, but Brenda held it behind her. "Give it back," whispered Libby angrily.

"She did find it first," said Ben, hurrying to Libby's side.

"See?" said Brenda smugly.

"I mean Libby found it first," said Ben in a low voice. "Give it back, Brenda."

"You can't make me!" snapped Brenda.

Libby sank down on the couch, her head down. She felt as though a million eyes were on her. Perspiration prickled on her forehead. "Let her keep it, Ben."

"Then you take mine and I'll find another one," said Ben, pushing an orange paper into Libby's limp hand.

"I'll find my own," said Libby, jumping up and pushing the paper back into Ben's hand. With her head high, she walked around the room, looking with great care. She just couldn't be the last one to find a paper! Out of the corner of her eye she saw the only other person still looking for a paper. With a shout of delight he hurried to the group and sat down. Libby's face flushed red, but she continued to hunt until finally she saw the last one tucked behind a picture on the wall near the snack bar. She hurried to the group and sat beside Susan.

Connie stood before the group, her hands folded, a bright smile on her lips. "As you all know, it's almost Thanksgiving. This is the time we set aside to remember all our blessings. We can be thankful for our homes, our food, and our clothing. We're thankful for friends, for families. One of the most important things we are to be thankful for is that Jesus can be a Savior to each of us."

Libby listened, trying to understand what Connie was saying.

"We have our Bibles," continued Connie, lifting her Bible high. "This is God's Word. Many people in other countries can't have a Bible to enjoy. Thank God we do. God speaks to us through this Word. The papers you have in your hands have Scriptures written on them that I thought would be good for us to read tonight." She looked right at Libby and smiled. "Would you read your Scripture first, Libby?"

Libby flushed, fumbled her paper, dropped it.

66

Brenda groaned.

Libby glared at her.

"Read it, Libby," said Susan, nudging Libby in the ribs.

"We don't have all day," said Brenda, scowling.

"We have plenty of time," said Connie pleasantly. "Read it, Libby."

With trembling fingers, Libby turned the paper right side up. "Ephesians 4:32. Be ye kind one to another . . . forgiving one another."

Brenda giggled. *"She* doesn't know how to be kind."

Libby knotted her fists and glared at Brenda.

"Quiet, Brenda," whispered Joe, poking her between the shoulder blades.

"Ignore her," said Susan in Libby's ear.

Libby forced herself to listen to Connie. Now and then she caught a word, but mostly she was thinking of Brenda's meanness.

By the time Joe was to read his Scripture, Libby had herself in hand. She listened attentively as Joe read a Scripture that Libby had heard Kevin recite.

"John 3:16," read Joe. "For God so loved the world, that he gave his only begotten Son, that whosoever believeth in him should not perish, but have everlasting life."

Libby's heart beat a little faster as Connie exclaimed excitedly about how wonderful God's great love was. She said that God loved each boy and girl listening to her. Libby frowned. Did God love her? She shrugged. This was just another of the strange things she had to put up with in her new foster home.

"Let's bow our heads and close our eyes and pray,"

said Connie softly. She prayed for God to bless each person, to show them all what to be thankful for at Thanksgiving time.

Libby felt strange as Connie continued praying that each boy and girl would live for Jesus every day. Just how would a person live for Jesus? Libby wrinkled her forehead. She'd never been around people who prayed the way Connie and the Johnsons did.

Just then Susan nudged Libby again. "We're going upstairs for hot cocoa and cookies," she said as she stood waiting for Libby. "Connie's cocoa is delicious!"

Self-consciously Libby followed Susan upstairs. She stood in line behind Susan at the table. Several of the kids came around them and tried to get acquainted with Libby. She could barely answer them. Why couldn't she be friendly? She couldn't even manage a smile. Soon the kids just drifted away.

Libby picked up her cocoa and walked to a corner of the room away from everyone else. Thankfully she sipped her cocoa. She looked up to find Brenda walking toward her. Libby quickly moved to another part of the room. Wildly she searched for Susan or Ben. She couldn't see them. Joe was standing with two boys near the television set.

Just as Libby took another sip of cocoa someone bumped her arm. Hot cocoa spilled down her green checked pullover and onto the thick gold carpet. She turned around to find Brenda gloating in triumph.

"You pushed me," whispered Libby.

Brenda grinned in satisfaction as she sidled over to stand near a group of kids. "Look what *she* did now," cried Brenda, pointing at Libby. "She is so clumsy."

Libby's mouth gaped. How could Brenda be so mean?

"Don't let it worry you, Libby," said Connie, rushing to her with a towel and a damp cloth. "As long as you're not hurt. Accidents happen to the best of us."

"It wasn't an accident," cried Libby, her pointed chin sticking out defiantly. "Brenda pushed me."

"She did?" asked Connie uncertainly as she looked across the room at Brenda.

"But, how could I?" asked Brenda innocently. "I'm way over here."

"You did do it," screamed Libby, rushing toward Brenda.

Ben and Susan grabbed Libby. "Calm down," whispered Ben. "We'll settle it later."

Frustrated tears filled Libby's eyes. What could they settle? No one ever believed her. Brenda would never admit her guilt. Never!

TEN
A visit from Miss Miller

Libby sat hunched in the blue chair by the family room fireplace. She was waiting for Miss Miller. Vera and Miss Miller were in the study, discussing Libby.

During the week and a half since Connie's party Libby had tried extra hard to stay out of trouble. Vera had had a long talk with her about how to behave at a party and how to apologize to someone when you spilled cocoa all over their gold carpet. Libby sighed as she leaned her head against the soft back of the chair. She'd finally stopped trying to convince them that Brenda had bumped her arm to make her spill the cocoa. It wasn't worth the struggle to convince them she was telling the truth. The corners of Libby's mouth drooped. Would Vera report all that to Miss Miller?

Libby leaped up and hurried to the window. A soft snow was falling, covering the ground in a beautiful white blanket. She leaned her forehead against the cool glass. Would Vera give Miss Miller a bad report? A nervous shiver ran down Libby's spine. Rex came bounding around the house, making tracks in the snow that were soon covered with fresh snow.

Slowly Libby walked back to the blue chair. Nervously she rubbed her hands down her jeans. Tomorrow was Thanksgiving. She had helped bake pumpkin pies and the apple pies that Vera said Grandpa liked so well. They'd all worked on making the house spotless.

Would Miss Miller insist on taking Libby with her today? Would she miss meeting Grandpa and Grandma Johnson? Kevin, Susan, and Ben had talked constantly about them. Kevin was especially excited about suprising them with Libby. She had been practicing over and over in front of her mirror. "I'm glad to meet you, Grandma and Grandpa," she muttered to herself, faking a smile.

"You can go in now," said Vera, coming into the family room, smiling warmly. "Miss Miller and I had a very nice visit."

Libby took a deep breath and walked with squared shoulders to the study.

Miss Miller greeted Libby happily, then motioned for her to sit down. "I like your hair short," she said. "That style is perfect on you."

Libby folded her hands in her lap and stared at her toes.

"Mrs. Johnson tells me you seem to fit right in the family," said Miss Miller, folding her hands on the big oak desk.

Libby looked up in surprise.

"Does that surprise you?" asked Miss Miller, her blue eyes twinkling. "She did tell me about a few differences of opinion that you've had with the kids,

but she said it wasn't anything they couldn't handle."
She smiled. "I'm glad to hear it, Libby. This is a special family. And you're a special girl."

Libby managed a small smile.

The rest of the interview went smoothly. Libby answered each question easily. It was a relief to know she wasn't being sent back.

"One more thing, Libby," said Miss Miller, studying the pencil she held.

A shiver ran down Libby's spine. "Yes?"

"I received a phone call from your mother two days ago."

Libby gasped. Her heart skipped a beat. Did Mother want her back again?

"Your father was killed in a car wreck last month. I'm sorry, Libby."

Libby felt almost guilty in her relief. Mother didn't want her back again. The news about her father didn't seem real to her. She didn't know him; he was a stranger.

"She also said if things work out right she wants you to spend Christmas with her."

Libby sat very still, her eyes on Miss Miller's hands.

"Would you like that, Libby?"

Libby shrugged sullenly. What would it matter if she wanted to or not? If they decided to make her go, she'd have to. Maybe Mother would insist on keeping her, only to desert her again in a few weeks.

Miss Miller stood up. "You can think about it. I'll be back sometime during the first part of December. You can tell me then."

Libby nodded, the ache in her heart worse.

"Walk with me to the door, Libby," said Miss Miller

brightly. "Tell me, have you made friends with that goose?"

"No," mumbled Libby, walking obediently beside Miss Miller.

"He greeted me when I got out of the car, but Kevin shooed him away."

Miss Miller slipped on her dark red coat and black boots. "Mrs. Johnson tells me you like the other animals and do a good job taking care of them. She said you've done an especially good job doctoring Snowball."

Had Vera told Miss Miller it was Libby's fault that Snowball had been hurt?

"Won't you stay for coffee?" asked Vera, hurrying into the hall.

"No thanks, Mrs. Johnson. I have three more calls to make before I can go home."

"Kevin's down in the basement, so I'll walk you to the car to keep our friendly goose from molesting you," said Vera, laughing as she slipped on her coat and boots.

"Thanks. I'm with Libby about that goose," said Miss Miller.

Libby watched through the long, thin window beside the heavy front door as Vera walked Miss Miller to the car. They talked a while, then Miss Miller drove away.

Vera hurried back to the house, wind blowing her blonde hair across her pretty face, snow making white spots on her. Libby opened the door, then closed it after Vera.

Libby waited expectantly, a chill crushing her heart.

"Miss Miller told me about your father. I'm sorry, Libby."

Libby shrugged as Vera hung up her coat and pulled off her boots.

"She also told me your mother wants you to spend Christmas with her," said Vera in a tight voice. "Do you want to?"

"I don't know," answered Libby stiffly. "Do you want me to go?"

"If you want to, Libby."

"She might want me back."

Vera was quiet for a long time. "I know."

The grandfather clock bonged, startling both of them.

Libby ran up the stairs. Did Vera want her to leave? Libby flung herself across her bed. Maybe it would be better to live with Mother. At least then Libby wouldn't be an aid kid. She wouldn't be anything!

ELEVEN
Lost in a snowstorm

Libby crept stealthily downstairs on Thanksgiving morning. No one else was up yet. It was still dark out. She put on her snowboots, her warm jacket with the hood, and red and black mittens. Her eyes were swollen from crying. Everytime she thought of going to Mother for Christmas she started crying. What should she do? Go? Stay? She didn't want to go, but she didn't want to stay if she wasn't wanted.

Quietly she opened the back door and stepped outside. It was light enough to see. She walked slowly toward the horse barn. At least she didn't have to worry about Goosy Poosy. He was still locked in the chicken house until Kevin turned him loose.

A horse nickered as she flicked on the barn light. Slowly she walked from stall to stall, talking to each horse. At Snowball's stall she stopped the longest. "Morning, Tessy. Morning, Snowball. Happy Thanksgiving. I'll help Ben give you a big feast after a while." She visited with them a little longer, then slowly walked out of the barn.

Snowflakes swirled around her, melting against her face. The big black and tan collie ran to Libby, wagging his tail in delight.

"Morning, Rex. Will you go for a walk with me?" Libby hugged him tightly, glad for his company.

With her hand on Rex's head Libby walked toward the trail where she and Ben went riding each day. The sky lightened.

Just as Libby reached the far side of the barn someone called her name. She turned in surprise to see Susan running toward her. Libby sighed. At least she wouldn't have a chance to think about Mother.

"You're sure out early, Libby," said Susan breathlessly, her face pink. "Couldn't you sleep either? I'm so excited about Grandma and Grandpa coming! They haven't been here for six months. Today they're coming!"

Libby leaned into the wind as she walked beside Susan along the trail. Sometimes it was fun to be with her. Sometimes it wasn't.

"Mom said you might go see your mother for Christmas," said Susan, walking backward to shield her face from the wind. "Are you going?"

"I don't know." Libby rested her hand on Rex's head to draw comfort from the friendly dog.

Susan stuck out her tongue and caught a snowflake on it. "I know where a fox den is. Want to see it?"

"Sure," said Libby, glad to think about something else.

Susan left the trail and ran among the naked trees, calling for Libby to follow.

Libby dashed after her, her heart light for the moment. It was fun with Rex running beside her and

Susan in front, leading the way to the fox den. Libby blinked snow off her eyelid.

"Hurry up, slowpoke," called Susan, turning with a laugh.

Libby followed, puffing and panting. She wasn't used to this much exercise. "Wait, Susan."

"Slowpoke! Slowpoke!" sang out Susan, laughter floating back to Libby through the falling snow.

Libby strained her eyes to see Susan through the snow. She couldn't see even a movement. Fearfully Libby ran in the direction she'd seen Susan go. Where was Susan? She wouldn't leave Libby alone in the woods, would she? Maybe she wanted to get even for all the mean things Libby had done and said to her. Libby shivered. Susan wouldn't leave her behind.

Libby reached the top of the hill, panting for breath. Rex spotted a rabbit and raced away, barking merrily. Libby's heart beat faster. "Rex, come back!" she called frantically. "Susan! Where are you?" Libby listened. Rex had stopped barking. Snowflakes swirled around Libby. She shivered. "Susan?" Silence. "Susan!" Silence, then a distant bark of a dog. Libby shivered with fear.

Frantically she dashed to look behind a giant tree, then dashed to another and another. Her heart raced. "Susan! Rex! Where are you?"

Panting for breath, Libby leaned against a tall, rough oak. That Susan! Why was she doing this? Hot tears stung Libby's eyes. She blinked hard, determined not to cry. Angrily she shoved away from the tree and looked around her. The snow swirled too fast for her to see at any distance. She raced from tree to tree, looking for Susan. This silly game of hide-and-seek was making Libby more frightened by the minute. When she got a hold of Susan, she'd punch her in the nose hard enough to break it! "Susan!" Was she running just ahead of Libby, staying out of reach to tease? "Susan! Come here this minute!"

The dead silence struck fear to Libby's heart. "I won't look for her another minute," she muttered, straining to see ahead. Which way to the house? Cold shivers raced up and down her spine. She cupped her hands around her mouth. "I hate you, Susan Johnson! I hate you more than I hate Brenda Wilkens."

Scalding tears streamed down Libby's cold face. Angrily she jabbed them away. She'd find her own way home. Susan could stay and play her stupid game!

Taking a deep, shaky breath Libby turned slowly, looking all around, trying to decide which way to go. Finally she broke off a small branch and stuck it in the ground under a tree. "Now I'll know where I started from in case I have to come back here and start again." The sound of her voice was loud on the quiet hill.

Slowly she walked down the hill, trying to find anything familiar. A pain stabbed her side. She rested until it went away, looking around fearfully in case a wild animal was creeping up on her. The snowfall had lightened, but the wind had increased, whistling through the trees and blowing relentlessly against Libby's thin frame. Libby shivered, hunching against the wind. She forced herself to walk on until she was sure she'd come in the wrong direction. Where was the trail? She was numb from cold. Slowly, with sagging shoulders, she turned and walked back in the direction she'd come until she found the branch poking from the ground. She squared her shoulders and walked down another direction, her legs rubbery from being so tired. Where was Rex? Had Susan taken him with her? Or had he tired of chasing rabbits and gone home?

She trudged on until she reached an open field. Frustrated tears streamed down her cheeks as she turned and walked back the way she'd come. She found her starting place and sank down on the cold, snowy ground and leaned her head against the rough oak. Were the Johnsons wondering where she was? Would they search for her? Would she ever be found? Slowly she pushed herself up. The snow had stopped falling. A weak sun came out. She shivered so hard her teeth chattered.

Painfully she walked down another way until she encountered a fence. In frustration she bit her lower lip to keep from sobbing aloud.

Wearily Libby made her way back to her starting point and started down yet another way. She walked until she wanted to give up and lie down next to a tree and fall asleep. That Susan! She was in for it now! At the sight of the trail Libby stopped in excited surprise. She covered her mouth and slowly shook her head. She'd found the trail! She knew where she was!

Excitedly she dashed down the trail and around a bend. She stopped in surprise at the sight of Ben astride Star.

"Where have you been?" he asked in concern. "We have been looking and looking."

Libby stood with her fists on her hips, her eyes blazing. "Why don't you ask that sister of yours where I've been?"

Ben kicked his feet out of the stirrups and slid to the ground. "What about Susan? She's gone too. Have you seen her?"

Fear wriggled down Libby. Had Susan been playing a game? Had she been hurt? Where was Susan?

Quickly Libby told Ben what had happened.

"The fox den? But that's way over that direction." He looped the reins over a branch. "Come on!" He ran off the trail, calling Libby impatiently.

Bone-weary, Libby raced after Ben. Her breath came in short gasps. The air was cold in her lungs. "Wait! Wait, Ben," she gasped, sinking to the ground, fighting for air.

"We can't wait," he said, dashing to her and roughly hauling her to her feet. "We've got to find Susan."

With her last ounce of strength, Libby followed Ben around tangled underbrush and over fallen logs.

"There she is," said Ben in a strangled voice.

Libby's heart dropped to her feet as she saw the crumpled heap of the small girl. A bitter taste filled Libby's mouth as she knelt beside the still girl.

"Susan," whispered Ben, kneeling beside his sister. "Susan." He carefully lifted her head onto his knees.

Slowly Susan opened her eyes. "Where's Libby?"

"I'm here," whispered Libby, her eyes large.

"I called and called and called and you wouldn't come," said Susan hoarsely.

"What happened?" asked Ben anxiously.

"I twisted my ankle and fell and hit my head against a tree. It knocked me out for a while. When I came to I called to Libby. She wouldn't come." Susan's eyes filled with tears. "Benjy, I'm so cold. Take me home."

Tears stung Libby's eyes as she and Ben made a

chair with their arms and maneuvered Susan onto it. Slowly they made their way back to Star. Libby patiently explained to Susan about getting lost and thinking Susan was to blame.

"I'm sure sorry, Susan," said Libby as they hoisted Susan onto Star's back. "I should've known you wouldn't be so mean."

"I'm sorry for thinking you were being mean to me," said Susan, smiling weakly down at Libby.

Libby blinked back happy tears as she walked on one side of Star and Ben on the other. Everything was going to be all right.

TWELVE
A visit from Brenda

Libby poked her head into Susan's bedroom. "Want company?" she asked with a smile.

"I'll say!" exclaimed Susan, propping her head up with one hand.

Libby sat Indian-style at the foot of Susan's bed. "I just finished putting the candles on Ben's birthday cake."

Susan sighed. "December 11, Ben's 13th birthday. A teenager. Won't you like it when we're thirteen?"

"That won't be for another year," said Libby, picking up a stuffed turtle and tracing around its plaid back. "You should've seen the people that came today for Christmas trees. I'll be glad when your ankle is well enough so you can go along."

"I will too." Susan pushed herself to a sitting position. "I'm glad you're helping Ben with his Christmas tree business. He sure couldn't do it alone."

"I like helping." Libby picked up a small teddy bear. "I'm happy we're finally friends, and a *family.*

Grandma and Grandpa loved you too," said Susan with a satisfied smile. She pushed her red-gold hair out of her face. "You're a great sister. It's fun playing games with you and having you come talk to me."

"I've been trying extra hard to be nice," said Libby shyly.

"Remember that Scripture you read at Connie's party? 'Be kind one to another.' I've been praying that Jesus will help me to be kind and not impatient. He has helped me. Why don't you pray that you'll be as good as you want to be?" Susan's blue eyes were very serious.

"I didn't think about it," said Libby, rubbing the brown fur on the teddy bear. "I thought praying was just something your family and church people did."

"*Everyone* can pray," said Susan, leaning forward earnestly. "It's only talking to Jesus."

Libby dropped the teddy bear and picked up a pink mouse. "I could try it sometime."

Susan settled back down on her pillow. She was supposed to be resting so that she could go down for Ben's birthday dinner. "Has Ben guessed any of his presents?"

Libby giggled. "No. He sure has tried. He keeps picking them up and shaking them."

Susan sat quietly. Libby could hear Rex barking outside. Piano music floated upstairs.

"What are you going to do about Christmas?" asked Susan, her eyes very serious.

Libby clutched the pink mouse tighter. "I don't want to think about it." Everytime the thought of spending Christmas with Mother had forced its way into her mind, she'd pushed it out.

"Stay with us for Christmas," begged Susan. "I want you to."

"I have two more weeks before Christmas. I'll decide later." Libby's mouth went dry.

Susan pulled a wrinkled paper from under her pillow. "Have you learned your piece for the Christmas program yet?"

"Most of it," said Libby proudly. She'd never taken part in a church Christmas program before. It was scary, but fun. She was glad Susan would be in the program too.

"Connie gave me a long piece to recite," said Susan, smiling. "She knew I wanted an extra long piece." She held out the paper. "Will you help me learn it?"

Libby took the wrinkled paper and listened while Susan quoted the first stanza. Patiently she helped her say it all. When Susan was halfway through the second time Brenda Wilkens walked in.

"I came to bring you something, Susan," said Brenda, completely ignoring Libby. "It's a book of crossword puzzles."

"Thank you," said Susan stiffly. "I do like crossword puzzles." Joe and Brenda had been to visit her twice since Thanksgiving.

Libby sat quietly at the foot of the bed, trying to keep her anger down. Brenda ignored her every time they were in the same room together.

"Does *she* have to stay in here while I visit you?" asked Brenda, motioning toward Libby.

Libby bit her lip to keep from saying something rude.

"I like to have Libby here," said Susan, frowning at Brenda, then smiling at Libby. "We're sisters."

Libby puffed out with pride.

"Not your real sister," said Brenda scornfully. "She's just living with you for a while."

"She's staying always," cried Susan.

"She's only an aid kid," snapped Brenda.

Libby leaped off the bed, anger flashing from her green eyes. Her short brown hair seemed to stand on end. "I don't like the smell in here, Sue. I'll be back when it's gone."

"Talk about smells!" snapped Brenda, glaring at Libby.

Libby lifted her pointed chin and sailed from the room. She raced down the carpeted stairs and into the family room, seething with rage.

"What's the rush?" asked Vera, turning from playing the piano.

"Nothing," said Libby, sinking down on the blue chair near the fireplace.

"You and Susan aren't fighting again, are you?"

"No. Brenda's with her."

"I didn't see Brenda come in," said Vera, frowning. "She should have let me know she was here. I guess I was too absorbed in my piano playing." She turned back to the piano. "I can't get this part right and I have to play it Sunday morning in church."

The music drifted through the room, soothing Libby until her anger was gone. How she would like to play as well as Vera!

When the song was finished Vera stood up. She pulled her red sweater down over her red pants and walked toward Libby. "That was better. I believe I have it now."

"I liked it," said Libby softly. She wanted to tell Vera it was the most beautiful song she'd ever heard, but the words wouldn't come. Libby kept her eyes on Vera's black shoes as Vera sat down across from her.

"We got a letter from Grandma and Grandpa today," she said, chuckling. "They were still in shock about us having a new girl. Kevin really laid it on thick with his surprise."

Libby laughed, remembering how embarrassed she'd been on Thanksgiving when Kevin had presented her to his grandparents as a big surprise.

"They send you their love," continued Vera, crossing

her ankles. "They were very impressed at the way you and Ben rescued Susan.

Libby flushed.

Vera fingered the chain necklace around her neck. "Have you decided about visiting your mother at Christmas?"

Libby stiffened. What did Vera want her to do? If only she knew!

A log crackled in the fire. The grandfather clock bonged the half hour.

"Miss Miller called this morning. She said she'll be out next week, that she couldn't make it this week," said Vera, clearing her throat. "She will need an answer then."

Libby kept her voice very controlled. "Do you want me to go?"

"It's up to you, Libby. It's a decision you'll have to make on your own." Vera locked her fingers together in her lap. "A mother wants her child with her, especially at the special time of Christmas."

A knot settled in Libby's stomach. She pressed her hands against her legs. Was Vera saying that she should go to Mother for Christmas? Did Vera want her out of the house?

Susan's bell tinkled, signaling she needed something. Libby jumped up. "I'll go." She didn't wait for even a nod of approval, but sped upstairs. She would not think about Mother now!

Susan was sitting up in bed, her face flushed, frowning. "Where did you put the copy of my Christmas piece?" she asked impatiently.

"I dropped it right on your bed," said Libby, looking around on the covers, under them, around the stuffed animals, under them. "I left it right here." She peeked under the bed. Susan's blue fluffy slippers and her stuffed skunk were the only things under it. Libby reached for the skunk and pulled it out. "It's got to be here, Sue," she said as she laid the skunk beside the plaid turtle.

"Brenda wanted to hear me say it, but I couldn't find the copy," said Susan, shaking the covers up high and looking under them again. "Are you sure you didn't take it with you?"

"I'm sure," said Libby, looking around the room. "Where's Brenda now?"

"She had to use the bathroom. She'll be right back." Susan poked her hand under her pillow and pulled it out empty. "Where could it be?"

"I don't know," said Libby, dropping on all fours to look better under the bed.

"You can stop pretending," said Brenda icily as she stepped into the room. "I found it."

"Where?" cried Susan.

Libby leaped to her feet. "Pretending what?" she cried.

"I thought I saw *her* take it when she left," said Brenda, walking to the edge of the bed. "So I looked in her room. I found this on her bed." Brenda opened her hands and dropped the paper. Small pieces of ripped papers fluttered to the bed over Susan's legs.

Susan covered her mouth, her eyes fixed on Libby in disbelief.

Libby gasped. She touched the torn paper, shaking her head helplessly, hopelessly.

"Libby?" asked Susan in a strangled voice.

Giant tears filled Libby's eyes and rolled down her cheeks.

"I told you she was no good," said Brenda smugly. "I told you no aid kid was good. She only pretends to be your friend."

Libby faced Brenda angrily. "You did it," she whispered hoarsely, shaking her finger under Brenda's nose. "You did it!"

"How could I? I've been here all the time," said Brenda, her nose high in the air. "Why on earth would *I* do such a thing? Susan's my friend."

"She did not do it, Libby," said Susan coldly. "She has been here all the time. You did it."

Libby was too heartbroken to deny it. How could Susan think she'd do such a thing?

"You're mean, Libby," cried Susan, shaking her finger at Libby. "I'm glad you're not really my sister."

Libby fled to her room, tears rushing down her cheeks, her heart almost breaking in two.

THIRTEEN
A surprise call

Restlessly Libby walked from one room to another. She was the only one inside. Vera and Susan were doing last-minute Christmas shopping. Chuck and the boys were working outdoors.

Libby stopped by the Christmas tree standing tall in the living room. The sleigh ride out to choose the tree had made her feel a little better. For a little while she'd been able to forget the lecture and the punishment she'd received for tearing up Susan's paper with the Christmas recitation on it. For a week she'd had to go straight to bed after dinner and had to miss all the wonderful family fun for that week.

She picked up a piece of tinsel that had fallen and draped it carefully over a branch.

Brenda *had* torn up Susan's paper, but nobody would believe Libby. Ben's birthday celebration had been ruined. Even as she thought about it, a large hand seemed to be squeezing her heart until all the blood was wrung from it. Tears filled her eyes. Impatiently she blinked them away.

Listlessly she walked to the far corner of the living

room where Kevin had set up the nativity scene. On the night of the Christmas program at church she'd seen this same scene, only with real people. Ben had been a shepherd. Libby touched the baby Jesus. It made her think of Susan's recitation. She'd stood in front of the church and said her piece with feeling and enthusiasm. Libby had been so proud of her. Libby had mumbled her recitation, stumbling over the last line.

Impatiently Libby pushed thoughts of the Christmas program out of her mind as she walked back to the Christmas tree. With her toe she nudged a red gift until she could read the label. Her heart skipped a beat. It was for her! What could it be? How could she wait two more days? Nothing else could happen to ruin her Christmas, could it?

At least she didn't have to go to see Mother for Christmas. Miss Miller had called Monday, saying that Mother had gone to Australia and would be gone at least a year.

The phone rang, startling Libby. She answered it.

"Libby, this is Brenda Wilkens."

Libby wanted to fling the phone down.

"I have a Christmas gift for you and the Johnson family, but I can't bring it over. Would you walk over and get it?"

"Why should I?"

"I'm really sorry for being mean, Libby," said Brenda in her most persuasive voice.

Libby couldn't believe her ears.

"At Christmas time we are all to be nice to each other. I want to be nice to you, Libby, and be friends if you'll let me. Will you come get the gift?"

Libby hesitated, then finally agreed. It would be

better to be friends. Maybe then Brenda would confess to tearing up Susan's paper. Then everything would be right again.

Feeling happy for the first time since Ben's birthday, Libby hurried into her outdoor clothes.

She trudged down the snow-covered driveway, looking behind her frequently for Goosy Poosy. At the end of the driveway she sighed in relief. She looked toward the Wilkens house, thinking how beautiful it looked, standing on the hill. A large pine tree stood tall and green against the snow.

The cold wind blew against Libby, making her shiver. As she walked she felt like singing. Brenda would confess and all would be well.

Libby hurried up on the front porch, her eyes bright. She pressed the doorbell. The melody drifted through the house. Libby waited expectantly. Would Brenda really be nice? Or would she find something to say or do to be mean? Libby rang the doorbell again, listening to the melody in the quiet house. A dog in the backyard barked. Libby slapped her mittened hands together and stomped her feet to keep warm. Impatiently she rang the doorbell again. Why didn't Brenda answer? It was so quiet inside, almost as if no one was home. Had Brenda left suddenly? Or was she inside, laughing gleefully at keeping Libby waiting in the cold? One more time Libby pressed the doorbell, keeping her finger on it a long time.

"Where are you, Brenda?" she muttered impatiently. She sighed in disgust, then slowly walked off the porch and down the long driveway to the road. Snowflakes drifted down, the wind swirling them around Libby. What mean trick was Brenda planning this time?

The ditches on both side of the road were filled with grimy snow. Libby kicked a can off the side of the road into the ditch. That Brenda!

Barking happily, Rex ran down the driveway to meet Libby. "Hi, boy." She patted his head, looking anxiously around for Goosy Poosy. He wasn't in sight. Libby walked through the snow to the swing and pushed it high. It swung up, jerked, and swung back down.

Goosy Poosy honked in the backyard, startling Libby. She dashed to the front door and rushed inside. The warmth wrapped around her. Slowly she pulled off her boots and her coat, shaking the snow off. Why had Brenda called her if she hadn't intended to answer the door?

By the time on the grandfather clock Libby knew Vera and Susan would be home soon. Had they bought Christmas gifts for her?

Libby plugged in the Christmas lights, enjoying the many colors shining among the branches of the tree. Again she peeked at the tag on the large red package. It really was for her. It looked so fancy beside the things she'd wrapped for the family.

She touched the package with the tip of her toe, yearning to snatch it up and rip off the paper. The rule that no one touched any of the presents, only looked at them, stopped her. She hugged herself, shivering with anticipation.

Libby walked to the family room. She ran her fingers over the piano keys, wishing she could make music like Vera.

Suddenly the stillness was interrupted by everyone coming into the house at once.

"You can't see what I have right here," said Susan, holding a bag up high in front of Libby.

"What?" asked Libby, reaching playfully for the bag.

"Don't tease, Susan," said Vera, taking the bag and pretending to give it to Libby.

"What's for supper?" asked Ben, flopping down on the couch. "I'm starved."

"I brought supper home with me," said Vera smugly. "You'll find a bucket of chicken and all the fixings on the table. Everyone wash up and we'll eat."

Libby laughed at the mad scramble that followed. It was good to have everyone around her.

"I took Goosy Poosy sledding with me," said Kevin as they sat eating chicken. "He loved it. I let him ride in front."

Everyone laughed. Libby could picture the friendly goose on the sled.

Susan and Vera talked about Christmas shopping until the meal was over. Libby listened excitedly, thinking of the fun she'd had shopping with Vera.

Later around the fireplace, Chuck read about John the Baptist. The phone rang, sharply, interrupting. Libby jumped. Vera answered.

Libby watched as the happy smile left her face. Ice settled around Libby's heart. What now? More trouble?

Vera hung up and turned to Libby with a stricken look. "Did you go to the Wilkenses' house today?"

Libby's stomach knotted. "Yes," she managed to say.

"Oh, Libby!" Vera sagged back in her chair; tears filled her blue eyes.

"What's wrong?" asked Chuck, taking Vera's hand and looking from her to Libby.

Libby locked her fingers around her knees, held her breath until her lungs ached, then slowly let it out.

"Mr. Wilkens said he had fifty dollars taken from his desk drawer. They found Libby's gloves on the floor by the desk," said Vera barely above a whisper.

Libby felt all the eyes on her. Slowly she lowered her head, pressing her face against her knees. Brenda had done it again, only this time Libby was in real trouble.

"This is serious, Elizabeth," said Chuck, clearing his throat. "Where is the money? Give it to us and we'll return it at once and set it straight with the Wilkenses."

Libby moaned, her heart almost breaking.

"They insist on us giving back the money AND sending Libby away," said Vera in agony. "If we don't, they'll call the police and press charges against Libby."

Libby lifted a stricken face, scalding tears streaming down her cheeks. She opened her mouth to deny everything, but no sound came out.

FOURTEEN
Nearing the end

Libby opened her eyes, dreading the day. Two more days on the Johnsons' farm, then back she'd go for Miss Miller to find her another foster home. Chuck and Vera had begged Mr. Wilkens to take fifty dollars from them and forget the whole thing. He wouldn't. He'd called Miss Miller and told her what Libby had done and that he was going to report it to the police if Miss Miller didn't get Libby immediately. Chuck had insisted they wait until after Christmas. Miss Miller had finally agreed, but only if Libby was brought in the day after Christmas.

Slowly Libby climbed out of bed. Tears filled her eyes as she realized this wasn't her room any longer. She dressed and walked slowly downstairs.

Vera's eyes were red-rimmed, her face white. Susan stood with a plate of pancakes in her hands, her face pale. Chuck and the boys were already at the table.

Libby blinked hard to keep the tears back as she sat down. The meal was quiet; even Kevin's usual chatter was silenced. They'd already told her they hated to see her leave, that they wanted her to stay and that they would do all they could to get her back. She wouldn't allow her hopes to be built up. She wouldn't see the Johnson family ever again. They'd soon forget her, maybe even get another foster child to take her place.

"The Parkses will be here soon to get their Christmas tree, Libby," said Ben, pushing back his chair. "Will you go with me?"

Libby nodded, knowing he was doing this because he knew it would be her last sleigh ride. He knew how much she loved riding behind the gray horses in the sleigh.

Snow sparkled on the ground as Libby stepped outside. She blinked against the brightness as she walked beside Ben to the barn. Goosy Poosy waddled beside Ben in the path Ben had shoveled. Libby could see her breath.

"I don't want you to leave," said Ben as they lifted the heavy harness down.

Libby worked beside Ben without answering him. She knew if she said anything she'd cry.

The sleigh bells jingled merrily as they flung the harness over the big horses. Just as they finished, the Parks family drove in.

Goosy Poosy greeted them with a lot of honking and wing flapping.

Libby couldn't help but smile at the excited Parks kids as they raced to the sleigh. She showed them where to sit and climbed in beside them. Mr. and Mrs. Parks sat on the front seat with Ben.

The swish of the runners over the hard-packed snow

and the merry jingle of the bells brought tears to Libby's eyes.

Ben started singing Jingle Bells. A lump in Libby's throat blocked the words back. She listened in agony as the others sang gaily. This was probably the last sleigh ride she'd ever have in her life.

Christmas day finally came.

"Let's make this a wonderful happy day for Elizabeth to remember," said Chuck as they gathered around the Christmas tree on Christmas morning. "We've prayed about getting her back when this whole thing is settled, so let's trust God for the answer."

Libby closed her eyes and forced the panicky feeling down. She wouldn't think about this being her last day with the Johnson family. It was Christmas Day, a day to be happy.

"Before we open our presents I want to read the Christmas story to you," said Chuck, sitting cross-legged on the carpet with his family around him. "Today is the day we honor Jesus' birthday." Chuck opened his Bible. "Jesus was born to be our Savior. He loves us even now that he is in heaven with his Father."

Libby listened carefully as Chuck read the story from Luke, of the shepherds watching their sheep when an angel came to announce the birth of Jesus. Libby pictured them going to find the baby by following the star, then bowing down and giving thanks for him. Love for Baby Jesus filled Libby's heart.

Vera prayed, thanking God for sending his Son and then praying that everything would work out just right for Libby. Libby's eyes smarted with unshed tears. She blinked hard, turning her head away as Chuck jumped up announcing gleefully that now was the time for opening presents.

Libby waited in excitement as Kevin unwrapped a football, Susan a purse, and Ben a wallet. Chuck handed Libby the red package she'd been dying to open. Eagerly Libby ripped off the paper and opened the box. Breathlessly she lifted out a red nightgown and robe. She clasped it to her in delight as Kevin opened another present.

One after another of the gifts were distributed and torn open. Libby already had around her, besides the red nightgown and robe, a game of Life, a white Bible, mittens, frilly underthings, and a long red and white Christmas dress that Vera had made just for her. Libby's eyes sparkled as she watched the others open and exclaim over their gifts. Libby had had as much fun buying and wrapping the gifts as the family did opening them.

"This is the last gift," said Chuck, taking a small, narrow box wrapped in shiny green paper with a gold ribbon and bow around it off a low tree branch. "Let me see." He grinned at Libby. "It's for our Elizabeth."

Libby's eyes misted with tears as she took the beautiful gift. She hadn't seen this one before. She opened it quickly, then gasped as she lifted out a gold locket on a long gold chain. Lovingly she looked at the fancy E carved on it.

"Open it," said Susan, crowding close to Libby.

"How?" asked Libby. She'd never owned a locket in her life. She'd never even touched one before.

"Here. Let me," said Ben, taking the delicate locket and springing it open. He handed it back to her with a grin.

"You're going to be surprised," said Kevin.

Libby looked with pleasure at the small pictures inside the locket. Vera and Chuck smiled up at her from the left side of the locket, the three kids from the right. Libby hugged it against herself as she breathed thank you to everyone.

"I'll put it on you," said Chuck, kneeling behind Libby.

She bent her head, lifting her hair as he put it around her slender neck and locked it. He put his arms around her and kissed her cheek. "We love you, Elizabeth."

Tears filled her eyes as she lovingly fingered the locket. It was the most precious gift she'd ever received. She'd wear it always. A hard knot hurt her stomach. It would be unbearable for the day to end. She'd pretend tomorrow would never come.

Vera jumped up, pulling her bathrobe tighter. "I am going to make breakfast. Who's hungry?"

"Me," cried Kevin, jumping up, his football under his arm. "I want French toast."

"French toast it is," said Vera, smiling as she hurried to the kitchen.

Chuck shook his head as he looked around at the disaster area around the Christmas tree. "Girls, clean up the papers, and boys, put the gifts in a neat order under the tree." Chuck put the Christmas record Libby had bought him on the stereo. In seconds beautiful Christmas music filled the room.

Libby put on her brightest smile and hid her broken

heart as she worked, ate breakfast, then hurried out to do the chores.

"Snowball," she said, hugging the white filly when no one was looking, "I will miss you so much!" Words caught in her throat and she couldn't speak. She opened each stall and let the horses out into the pen beside the barn. She hugged Apache Girl, then kissed Star right on the white mark. "Good-bye," she whispered, tears in her eyes.

"Ready to go, Libby?" asked Kevin, poking his head in the barn door. It was always the same. Kevin walked her to the house after chores to protect her from Goosy Poosy.

"Ready," said Libby, forcing her voice back to normal.

"I didn't let Goosy Poosy out of the pen today," said Kevin as they walked slowly through the snow to the house. "I wanted you to not have to be afraid of anything."

"Thanks," said Libby, smiling through tears.

"Soon we'll go sledding down the hill in back of the chicken house," said Kevin, kicking a clump of snow, sending it spraying into the air.

"OK." She'd been too busy with the Christmas tree business to go sledding. Ben had assured her there would be plenty of opportunities to go after Christmas.

Slowly Libby and Kevin walked around by the chicken house. Goosy Poosy honked and ran to the fence, flapping his wings indignantly to be let free.

"You'd have gotten over your fear of Goosy Poosy if you'd been here long enough," said Kevin, touching the goose through the wire fence. "Libby! I don't want you to leave!"

101

They walked to the patio. Libby absently rubbed the snow off the table. Kevin had told her about their summer cookouts. Pain squeezed her heart. She wouldn't be here for a summer cookout. With all her heart she wished she could stay. What good did it do to wish? She slapped snow off her mittens. Nothing ever went right in her life. Why should it now?

FIFTEEN
Leaving the family

Libby looked in disgust at her shabby suitcase. How could she fit her nice things into that? Why not just leave the nice things and take her rags? She'd be in rags again before long anyway. What foster family would be nice and give her pretty things except the Johnsons?

Slowly she sank down on her beautiful bed. It wasn't hers any longer. Fresh tears filled her eyes. Last night she'd cried herself to sleep.

Who would come live with the Johnson family now? Would Miss Miller know of another foster child to bring? Would Chuck say they'd been praying for just the right girl? Libby sniffed hard. She had been the right girl, only Brenda Wilkens had made it look as though she wasn't. Libby hugged Pinky tightly. Had Brenda done all the bad things that Libby had been blamed for? Libby shrugged. What did it matter now?

Libby kissed Pinky. She was leaving him behind for the next girl that lived here. "I don't want to leave, Pinky. I want to stay!"

Libby flung herself across the bed, her hair fluffy

around her face. Would her next foster parents let her hair grow long and straggly and put it back into braids?

Vera came in and stood beside the bed, large tears in her blue eyes. Libby sat up in alarm.

"Is it time to go already?" asked Libby in desperation.

"No. I just wanted some time alone with you." Vera sat down on the hassock and pulled Libby down beside her. "I love you, Libby. More than anything else, I want what is best for you. We're being forced to give you up for now at least. I want you to remember the things we've taught you here. Go to a new family with an open heart. If you love other people, you can't lose even if you're taken away from them. The love for them will always be with you."

Libby stared at Vera's long slender fingers.

"Libby, be loving to others. Give of yourself to others. Don't be afraid to care for people." She took Libby's clammy hands in hers. "The most important thing I want you to remember is that God loves you. Jesus wants to be your Friend, your personal Savior. Libby, do you love Jesus?"

Libby thought of the baby Jesus and she nodded yes.

"I'm glad, honey. If you love Jesus, he will be with you and help you. He loves you, Libby." Vera tightened her hold. "I want to pray with you one last time."

The knot in Libby's stomach was making her sick. She bowed her head next to Vera's. The prayer made Libby feel a little better. Just as Vera stood up, Susan came in with a large white suitcase in her hand.

"I want you to have this, Libby," she said, her voice breaking.

"But that's your birthday present from Grandma and Grandpa Johnson," said Libby. "You can't give it to me."

"Yes, I can, Libby. You're my sister." Susan turned away, crying.

Libby put her arms around the short girl and hugged her tightly. "You're the best sister I'll ever have." Libby wanted to tell her that she loved her and would never forget her. She longed to have something she could give Susan to show how much she cared, but she had nothing to give.

"Want some help packing?" asked Vera.

"I'll do it myself," said Libby, fighting more tears.

"Mrs. Wilkens called to make sure you were really leaving," said Vera, brushing a piece of lint off Libby's sleeve. "I told her you were going for now, but that we would try to get you back soon."

"I'll bet that made Brenda mad," said Libby gruffly.

Vera gave Susan a look and they both left. Libby knew they didn't believe Brenda had done any of the things that Libby had accused her of.

Libby hoisted the suitcase up onto her bed and opened the lid. It smelled new. As she packed each item Libby remembered how she'd felt when she'd received it. She lifted her new red and white Christmas dress off the hanger. She hadn't worn it yet. She rubbed her hand down the soft sleeve. Would she ever have a chance to wear it? Would her next foster parents ever go to church?

Libby picked up the cream sachet and rubbed a small amount on her wrists. It smelled so good. It had been nice of Susan to give it to her.

Finally she finished packing. She locked the suitcase

and plopped it down next to the door. One last time she looked around the pink and red room. Pinky sat forlornly on the bed. She saw the wet spots where her tears had fallen. "Good-bye, Pinky. I love you."

In anguish Libby dropped down on the large round hassock. That Brenda! Why had she done it? Why couldn't Libby convince the family that Brenda was guilty? Ben had said that maybe Libby had done all those things, and then forgotten she'd done them. He said he'd heard of that happening.

Slowly Libby picked up the suitcase and walked downstairs, the suitcase bumping her long, thin legs. The family waited at the bottom of the stairs, their eyes on Libby.

Ben took her suitcase, his hand touching hers. Libby wanted to hug him and tell him she'd never forget him.

Slowly they filed out of the house into the garage. Ben put the suitcase into the trunk of the car while Chuck opened the garage doors. Goosy Poosy honked loudly. Libby grabbed Kevin's arm and waited for the goose to come running. He didn't. His honking grew louder, more distressed.

"What is wrong with that goose?" asked Vera as she opened the car door.

"I'll go check," said Kevin, jerking away from Libby and running around the house. "What in the world! Come here, everyone! Come look at Goosy Poosy."

"What is it?" asked Chuck in concern.

Libby held onto Susan's arm as they followed close behind.

"Look!" exclaimed Kevin, pointing.

Everyone gasped, exclaiming in surprise. Goosy

Poosy was tied to the fence with a blue plaid tie and a bright red scarf. He honked hoarsely.

"Who did this?" asked Chuck, looking around accusingly.

"It sure wasn't Libby," said Susan, her blue eyes big. "It wasn't me either."

"Nor me," said Ben and Kevin together.

"Then who?" asked Vera, looking bewildered.

"Brenda Wilkens," gasped Libby. "It's just one more thing to blame on me."

"Do you suppose?" asked Vera. "That is my scarf and your tie, Chuck. How would she get them?"

"Poor Goosy Poosy," said Kevin, untying the scarf and tie. The goose shook his head, then swayed awkwardly over to the water pan.

Chuck scratched his head, "Something is certainly going on." He turned to Libby. "Do you really think Brenda did this?"

"Yes! I know she tore up Susan's paper before Christmas and I know she called me to come to her house. I didn't go in at all. I didn't take that money. And I sure didn't tie up Goosy Poosy."

"We'd better ride over to our neighbors and pay them a visit," said Chuck. "Vera, call Miss Miller and tell her we'll be late. Tell her we might not have to bring Libby in."

Libby almost shouted with glee. She climbed in the backseat of the car with the other three kids, listening to them chatter about what had happened and speculating on all the other things that had happened that Libby had been blamed for and hadn't done. Libby was too excited to join in. The muscles in her stomach tightened until she thought she was going to be sick.

The ride to the neighbors' house was short. The five Johnsons with Libby trooped up onto the porch. Chuck punched the doorbell. Libby shivered as the melody drifted faintly out to her.

Joe opened the door and stared in surprise.

"We want to talk to your parents and to Brenda," said Chuck, stepping inside, then making room for the others to come in.

Libby felt sorry for Joe. They'd been friends until Brenda had convinced him she had taken the fifty dollars. Joe looked scared as well as bewildered.

"It's OK, Joe," whispered Libby. "The mystery has been solved."

"It has?" he asked in surprise. "Are you giving back the money?"

"Tell your father we're here," said Chuck firmly.

Joe turned and hurried away, calling his dad.

Susan squeezed Libby's arm. Libby shivered in anticipation. The room was hot, too hot for coats. Chuck took off his and motioned for the others to do the same. He heaped them on the deacon's bench as Mr. Wilkens marched in to greet them.

"What is *this* all about?" he asked gruffly, looking from one to the other. He puffed his chest out. His face was red.

"We need to talk," said Chuck firmly.

Mr. Wilkens hesitated.

"It's about your daughter and mine. It concerns my family as well as yours."

Libby hugged her arms against her chest. Ben winked at her.

"Come into the family room," said Mr. Wilkens grudgingly. "The others are in there." He marched ahead, the six others bringing up the rear like a line of ducks going to the swimming hole.

Mrs. Wilkens greeted them hesitantly. Brenda flushed, then looked belligerently at Libby. Joe sat on the floor near the Christmas tree. They hadn't bought it from Ben.

Mr. Wilkens motioned for them to be seated, then sat beside his wife on the sofa.

Libby sat on the floor in front of Chuck's knees. She watched the fire flickering in the fireplace. She looked up at the big brass swords crossed above the mantle.

"We've come about our daughter's problem," said Vera.

Libby beamed. Daughter! She looked at the smug look on Brenda's face and for just a second fear tightened around her heart.

"You call this, this child, your daughter?" asked Mrs. Wilkens, waving her hand to indicate Libby. "I don't know how you can claim the likes of her. My, the trouble she has caused!"

"She didn't do it," said Ben sharply, then closed his mouth from the look Chuck gave him.

"Then who did?" asked Mr. Wilkens gruffly. "That fifty dollars didn't walk away by itself from my desk."

"Ask Brenda," said Vera, looking squarely into the girl's eyes.

Brenda lifted her dark eyes and stared right back.

Chuck leaned forward, also looking at Brenda. "Tell us about the phone call you made to Elizabeth two days before Christmas."

Mr. Wilkens puffed out his chest. "We've heard all we're going to hear on that subject." His eyes were hard.

Libby caught back a nervous giggle. Susan squeezed her arm. Kevin coughed.

"You went too far today, Brenda," said Chuck grimly. Brenda squirmed nervously.

"What do you mean by that?" asked Mrs. Wilkens.

"Libby is scared to death of our goose," explained Vera, resting her hands lightly on her black purse. "She has been from the day she first came."

"She only pretended to be afraid," cried Brenda, tossing her head so her dark hair bounced over her shoulder.

"No, she wasn't pretending," said Susan. "She was too scared to walk into the yard with Goosy Poosy around. Kevin always walked her to and from the barn for chores."

Libby watched in satisfaction as beads of perspiration popped out on Brenda's forehead.

"Will you get to the point of all this?" demanded Mr. Wilkens.

"You tell him, Brenda," said Chuck sternly.

"I have nothing to tell," she said icily.

"You see, Mr. and Mrs. Wilkens," said Chuck, leaning forward. "Brenda took a great dislike to Elizabeth right from the start. She has been doing small things and blaming them on Elizabeth just to get her in trouble. I hate to admit it, but I thought Elizabeth was to blame. I thought she'd done things by accident or had done them without remembering that she'd done anything." He squeezed Libby's shoulder. "Until today. Today I knew our girl hadn't tied up our goose. She couldn't have done it. We want to know if Brenda did it."

"Me! How could I? Why would I?" asked Brenda in shocked innocence.

"What is this nonsense about your goose?" asked Mrs. Wilkens, fumbling with the beads around her neck.

"Goosy Poosy was found tied up with my red scarf and Chuck's tie," explained Vera. "We were supposed to believe Libby did it. We knew she couldn't have." Vera looked from Brenda to her parents. "Brenda's been doing a lot of hateful things and blaming Libby. We've come to put a stop to it."

Brenda leaped to her feet, her eyes wild. "You can't blame me for anything. She did it." She pointed to Libby. "That aid kid did it."

"I did not!" cried Libby, scrambling to her feet. "You opened the gate and let out the sheep."

"I did not!"

"You cut off the bell rope and hid it in my jacket pocket."

Brenda clenched her fists. "I did not!"

"You tore up Susan's paper and *you* took that fifty dollars!" Libby's face was flushed, her eyes bright. "You called me and told me to come over here. I came, but I didn't go into the house."

"I didn't make a phone call," cried Brenda shrilly. "We were in town that day. Weren't we, Mother?"

"Of course we were. You were with me every minute, and you didn't call anyone." Mrs. Wilkens moved restlessly.

"What about a pay phone?" asked Chuck. "She could easily have used a pay phone."

"I didn't!" cried Brenda.

Joe leaped to his feet. "Yes, you did, Brenda. Remember? I saw you. I asked you who you'd called and you said you'd called Dad at his office."

"Ridiculous," sputtered Mr. Wilkens. "You're neither one allowed to call my office."

"She said she had," said Joe firmly. "Didn't you, Brenda?"

"No!" screamed Brenda, her knuckles white.

Mr. Wilkens jumped up, his face even redder. "I want you all out of my house this minute. Leave or I'll call the police."

"Go ahead and call the police," said Chuck, waving toward the phone beside the sofa. "But you'll have to report your own daughter."

Brenda gasped. Mr. Wilkens slumped back on the sofa beside his wife.

"You called me," said Libby, stepping close to Brenda. "You wanted me to come over here so you could put the blame on me for taking your father's money."

Brenda glared into Libby's face. "I hate you, aid kid. You're always hanging around Ben. He likes you better than he does me." Brenda stamped her foot. "You don't have anything. You're just an aid kid. Why should you live with them?" She waved toward the Johnsons. "They don't need you."

"Where's the money, Brenda?" asked Libby fiercely. "Get it and give it back."

"I'll never give it back. Never!"

"Brenda!" gasped Mrs. Wilkens, jumping up beside her daughter.

"What are you saying?" asked Mr. Wilkens, standing

beside his wife, his face very red.

Brenda covered her mouth and dashed from the room, her long dark hair streaming behind her.

Mrs. Wilkens burst into tears. Mr. Wilkens cleared his throat.

"We'll see that she's punished for this," he said.

Vera put her arm around Libby. "Love and punishment go together," Vera said softly.

"I'm sorry, Libby," said Joe awkwardly.

Libby smiled shyly at him. "It's OK now."

Chuck ushered his family to the door. Quietly they slipped on their coats and filed outdoors and climbed into the car. A dog barked in the backyard. A bird flew off the tall pine and disappeared in the distance.

"Libby, you get to stay!" cried Kevin, Susan, and Ben together.

Chuck looked over his shoulder and smiled. "Elizabeth Gail, we're taking you home."

"I'll call Miss Miller and tell her not to expect us," said Vera, smiling.

Libby leaned back against the car seat, a satisfied smile on her wide mouth.

SIXTEEN
Valentine's Day

Libby studied the desk calendar, her face puckered in a frown. Today was her twelfth birthday. Today was Valentine's Day. Today was the last day of her punishment. She turned away with a sigh and finished dressing. "Pinky, why can't I ever stay out of trouble?" Every day she promised herself that she wouldn't do anything or say anything that would get her into trouble. Three days ago she'd smashed all of Kevin's airplane models because he'd called her a Valentine sweetheart once too often. Kevin had been scolded for teasing her, but she'd had to go to bed early for the past three days.

She picked up Pinky. "Will I ever learn to be good?" she asked. She kissed his black nose and dropped him back on her bed.

She brushed her hair, poked a stubborn pocket down into her jeans, and hurried out of her room. It was Saturday. No school, she thought happily as she walked down the carpeted hallway to Susan's room.

She stuck her head in the doorway, then quickly stepped back. Susan was still asleep. Libby didn't dare wake her. She'd tried it before and Susan had been mad for a long time.

In the family room Libby slid onto the piano seat, pulled her music out from behind Vera's, and started practicing. She loved touching the right keys, making the correct melody. Vera had started just last month giving her piano lessons.

As she finished in one book and pulled out another, a large hand clamped onto her thin shoulder. She twisted her head to look, then smiled.

"Morning, Dad," she said, leaning her cheek against his hand.

"Happy birthday, sweetheart," said Chuck, kissing her. "Come into my study and talk to me for a while. I have an hour before I must go to the store."

He looked so serious that Libby's heart leaped. Slowly, she followed him. He indicated for her to sit on the sofa with him.

He took her hand. "Elizabeth, I've been praying for you for a long time. In fact, from the first time Miss Miller told us about you."

Libby kept her eyes on his hand. What was he going to say? Was he leading up to tell her she really didn't belong to the family?

"Elizabeth, you really belong to our family now. We can't adopt you, but we know that you'll stay with us until you're of age."

Libby nodded, relieved beyond words. She couldn't live without them.

"I want to talk to you about your personal relationship with Jesus. You've been in our family and church long enough to know that we each have a personal experience with Jesus." He reached for his Bible on the end table beside the lamp. "I know you love the baby Jesus. I want you to also love him as your Savior. I want you to belong to the family of God."

Libby's heart beat faster. She'd been thinking a lot about living for Jesus the way the others in the family and church did. Connie had said just last Sunday in Sunday school that each person had to accept Jesus as his or her own personal Savior, that a person couldn't live off his parents' relationship with Jesus. Libby picked a piece of Pinky's fur off her jeans and held it between her finger and thumb.

"Elizabeth, did you know that everyone has sinned? Everyone has done wrong?" asked Chuck, opening his Bible.

Libby nodded, knowing that she had done a lot of bad things she really hadn't wanted to do, but just couldn't help herself.

Chuck explained to Libby that because Adam and Eve had sinned in the Garden of Eden, everyone was born in sin. Because of sin, man would die and go to hell that had been prepared for only the devil and his angels. Libby nodded, saying Connie had told this in Sunday school class.

"God created us to love and serve him," said Chuck earnestly. "But, because of our sinful lives, he can't be friends with us. We must first have our sins taken away, then God can be our Heavenly Father." He told her of the crucifixion, then of Jesus being raised from the dead, and living in heaven with God.

"Jesus took your sins on himself, Elizabeth. He

116

wants you to give him all your sins so he can give you eternal life."

Libby's eyes filled with tears as she began to understand all he was telling her.

"You know how hard it is to be good, don't you?" asked Chuck, patting her head. "God gives his children strength to be good. Sometimes we forget to ask for his help, but he is always ready to help us."

A tear ran down Libby's cheek. "I want to be good like all of you. I want to be happy and love Jesus."

Chuck squeezed her hand. "Let's pray."

Chuck prayed, thanking God for Libby. Then she prayed too, asking Jesus into her heart. She tingled all over as she realized she really did belong to the family of God. She belonged to the Johnsons' family and to God's family.

Finally she lifted her tear-stained face. "I guess this means I have to try to love and forgive Brenda Wilkens like you've been telling us all along," she said, grinning.

"It sure does."

Libby shook her head helplessly. "Then Jesus is going to have to help me a lot."

Vera came in, tugging her bathrobe around her. "You are both early birds this morning."

"Morning, Mom," said Libby, kissing Vera's cheek. "I just asked Jesus to take away my sins and be my Savior." She made a face. "Now, I have to ask him to help me forgive Brenda Wilkens. And to *love* her."

"Oh, Libby!" exclaimed Vera, hugging Libby. "And on your birthday. That gives you two birthdays on the same day. The day you were born into this world and the day you were born into the family of God."

"Now Kevin will have something else to tease me about," said Libby, wrinkling her nose. "Oh, well. I guess I can take it."

"I guess you can," said Chuck. "And I guess that Kevin had better watch that teasing." He kissed her. "I've got to get ready for work."

Libby's heart swelled with pride as he walked toward the door. "Bye, Dad. See you later."

He turned and blew her a kiss. She knew he liked having her call him Dad. And Vera liked being called Mom. Libby couldn't remember when she'd started calling them Mom and Dad, but it sure made her feel good.

"Want to help bake your birthday cake?" asked Vera, her arm across Libby's shoulders as they walked toward the kitchen.

"Sure. A chocolate one."

While they mixed up the cake Vera said, "Miss Miller called last night. She wanted me to tell you happy birthday. Wasn't that nice of her to remember?"

Libby thought of all the bad times she'd given Miss Miller. She'd call her and tell her how sorry she was and thank her for finding her such a terrific family.

Vera smiled, bubbling with excitement. "Miss Miller said that she has a boy for us if we want him. He's eight years old and has red hair. Can you believe that? Red hair! And freckles. His name is Toby Smart."

Libby stood perfectly still, the spatula clasped tightly in her hand, chocolate cake batter dripping off the end. "Does that mean I have to leave?"

"Of course not! We've been praying for someone to fill our empty bedroom. Have you forgotten? Toby Smart will be that person. The other kids don't know yet, but won't they be excited? Especially Kevin."

"When's he coming?" asked Libby, excited too now that she knew she was staying in the family.

"Sometime next week."

"Can I tell the others about Toby Smart?"

"Sure," said Vera, pouring the cake batter into two round tins. "Open the oven door and I'll put these in." She slid them in. "You're a good helper, Libby, and I know you'll be a great helper to us when Toby comes."

A melody seemed to be bubbling inside Libby, ready to burst out. She was so happy!

Later that evening, after a dinner of fried chicken, mashed potatoes, corn, tossed salad, and fresh rolls, Libby looked happily around the table. The large chocolate cake with twelve fat red candles stood in the middle of the table, waiting for Libby to make a wish and blow out the candles.

"Happy Valentine's day, sweetheart," said Chuck, smiling.

"Happy birthday, valentine," said Kevin, grinning. He adjusted his glasses and said, "Oooppps. I forgot I wasn't supposed to tease you. Sorry."

Libby made a face at him, then smiled.

"Blow them out," said Susan impatiently. "We want to give you a present."

Libby looked at the buffet. There wasn't even one gift sitting on it.

"It's too big to put there." said Ben, grinning. "Hurry up, Libby."

Libby closed her eyes tight. "I wish our new brother Toby Smart will be happy with us right from the first day." She opened her eyes and blew. One candle stayed lit.

"You have a boyfriend," said Susan, shaking a playful finger. "Joe Wilkens. He sits with you in church every Sunday."

Libby wrinkled her nose at Susan, but couldn't get mad over any teasing today. Today was her special, special day. She blew out the last candle, excitedly anticipating her gift.

"I think, to keep us all from bursting with excitement, we'd better give Elizabeth her gift before we have cake and ice cream," said Chuck, pushing back his chair and standing up. "Come with me, everybody."

Libby was ready to die of curiosity.

"We must go outside to get it," said Vera as they followed Chuck to the back porch.

"What is it?" asked Libby as they all slipped on their coats.

"Wait and see," said Kevin, squirming excitedly.

"I'll tell her," whispered Ben, leaning close to Libby. "It's Goosy Poosy."

Libby shrieked. "You're kidding, Ben." She was still a little afraid of the friendly goose. At least at chore time she could now walk to and from the barn without Kevin as an escort. She hadn't had the courage to touch Goosy Poosy yet, but once he had rubbed his long neck against her leg and she hadn't fainted.

The wind blew against Libby as she stepped outdoors. Rex barked and joined them. Goosy Poosy was already in the pen, eating his grain.

Susan took Libby's arm as they walked through the snow. "It's a bike, Libby. A ten speed with everything."

"Stop teasing her," said Chuck, swatting playfully at Susan. "I want her to be surprised when she sees her motorcycle."

Everyone laughed gleefully. Chuck stopped outside the horse barn. Libby's heart raced. It must be something really big if they had to hide it in the barn.

Ben flipped on the light. Chuck led them down the aisle of the barn to the last stall. On the door hung a large red ribbon with a huge tag that said, "TO OUR DAUGHTER, ELIZABETH GAIL."

Libby blinked hard, then slowly opened the stall door. Snowball nickered and nuzzled her arm. Libby

turned to the family. "You mean she is for me? Snowball is for me?"

"Yes," said Vera, happy tears in her eyes.

"And look there," said Kevin, pointing outside the stall on a bale of straw.

Libby gasped. A saddle, bridle, and halter lay there with a tag saying, "From Susan, Ben, and Kevin."

Tears ran down Libby's flushed face.

"Now when you ride Apache Girl or Star, you'll have your own tack," said Susan, brushing tears from her eyes.

"And you can teach Toby how to ride," said Ben, smiling happily.

Libby looked at each one of her family for a long time without saying a word. She swallowed the lump in her throat and pressed her trembling hands to her heart. "I love you," she said. "I love you all very much."

ABOUT THE AUTHOR

Hilda Stahl was born and raised in the Nebraska Sandhills. When she was a young teen she realized she needed a personal relationship with God, so she accepted Christ into her life. She attended a Bible college where she met her husband, Norman. They and their seven children now live in Michigan.

When Hilda was a young mother with three children, she saw an ad in a magazine for a correspondence course in writing. She took the test, passed it, and soon fell in love with being a writer. She would write whenever she had free time, and she eventually began to sell what she wrote.

Hilda now has books with Tyndale House Publishers (the Elizabeth Gail series, The Tina series, The Teddy Jo series, and the Tyler Twins series), Accent Books (the Wren House mystery series), Bethel Publishing (the Amber Ainslie detective series, and *Gently Touch Sheela Jenkins,* a book for adults on child abuse), and Crossway Books (the Super JAM series for boys and *Sadie Rose and the Daring Escape,* for which she won the 1989 Angel Award). Hilda also has had hundreds of short stories published and has written a radio script for the Children's Bible Hour.

Some of Hilda's books have been translated into foreign languages, including Dutch, Chinese, and Hebrew. And when her first Elizabeth Gail book, *The Mystery at the Johnson Farm,* was made into a movie in 1989, it was a real dream come true for Hilda. She wants her books and their message of God's love and power to reach and help people all over the world. Hilda's writing centers on the truth that no matter what we may experience or face in life, Christ is always the answer.

Hilda speaks on writing at schools and organizations, and she is an instructor for the Institute of Children's Literature. She continues to write, teach, and speak—but mostly to write, because that is what she feels God has called her to do.

*If you've enjoyed the **Elizabeth Gail** series,*
double your fun with these delightful heroines!

Anika Scott

Fascinating stories about an
American girl growing up in Africa.

#1 The Impossible Lisa Barnes

#2 Tianna the Terrible

#3 Anika's Mountain

#4 Ambush at Amboseli

#5 Sabrina the Schemer

Cassie Perkins

Bright, ambitious Cassie discovers God
through the challenges of growing up.

#1 No More Broken Promises

#2 A Forever Friend

#3 A Basket of Roses

#4 A Dream to Cherish

#5 The Much-Adored Sandy Shore

#6 Love Burning Bright

#7 Star Light, Star Bright

#8 The Chance of a Lifetime

#9 The Glory of Love

You can find Tyndale books at fine bookstores everywhere.
If you are unable to find these titles at your local bookstore,
you may write for order information to:

Tyndale House Publishers
Tyndale Family Products Dept.
Box 448
Wheaton, IL 60189